# Twenty Years Together

'Queer love is not conventional – it was never afforded
that luxury. Holding hands on the sidewalk is a bolder move
than it should be. Finding our other half, building a family
and making a safe haven is what we strive for, but it is often a
struggle. *Twenty Years Together* is an enthralling novel of missed
connections and found companionship. It's about where we look
for love and chosen families. Tom Rob Smith has delivered a
classic love story for the modern era, where love is the
greatest hope and equality the greatest struggle'
**John-Paul Sarni**, writer and producer

'A gorgeous, funny and quietly revolutionary love story.
*Twenty Years Together* captures what it means to grow up and
grow older together; not in spite of being gay, but beautifully,
wholly because of it. Tom Rob Smith reminds us that queer
love can be messy and miraculous all at once'
**Gordon Greenberg**, Broadway and West End director and writer

'The warmth, the sharpness, the intelligence of every
character … The kinds of conversations we get to witness
between bright, sensitive people – and the life-defining decisions
that these two beautiful men have to make – are like gifts Tom
Rob Smith presents us with in his most delicate way. This book
is like a friend you love talking to, crying with, laughing with.
With powerful, innocent and always reflective dialogue, it cuts
to the big questions of: What is happiness? What is friendship?
What is marriage? *Twenty Years Together*, a beautifully self-
reflective novel, had me in tears from beginning to end'
**Juan Pablo Di Pace**, actor, writer, director

'As we now witness recently acquired LGBTQ freedoms
being challenged, Tom Rob Smith delivers this keenly observed
love story, which follows Danny and Luis as they navigate twenty
years together. From 1992 to a more embracing 2012 we observe
the burdens they've each carried from less accepting times
and the continued impact of these adversities. This brilliantly

affecting and often funny love story calls to mind the seminal
bildungsroman *A Boy's Own Story*. It is a joy to read'
**Michael Kaplan**, BAFTA-winning costume designer
(*Blade Runner, Star Wars, Fight Club*)

'*Twenty Years Together* is expansive yet intimate, expertly
crafted, charming, touching and constantly surprising; a
reminder of where the LGBTQ+ community has been,
where we are, and where we must remain'
**Alexis Gregory**, playwright (*Riot Act, FutureQueer, Smoke*)

'A beautiful and deeply moving book that
will stay with you for a very long time'
**Johann Hari**, writer and journalist

'*Twenty Years Together* is a tender portrait of two men who
love each other but do not know each other, because they do not
know themselves. Tom Rob Smith has captured the anatomy
of a long-term relationship with heartbreaking honesty. It is a
profound exploration of what it means to love and be loved, and
the pain that resides in a moment of fracture; a moment that
demands courage and unvarnished truths to rebuild and face
the terrifying beauty of finally being seen for the person you
were and the person you have become. It is a masterful story of
resilience, hope and love between two people building a life
on shared ground. It is a triumph of the spirit'
**Simon Oldfield**, curator and co-founder of Pindrop

'I love this book. It's quietly joyous and it's quietly
heartbreaking. *Twenty Years Together* captures the ordinary
heroism of loving someone for a lifetime in the most beautiful,
aching way. It's a novel of such gentleness and emotional
honesty it almost hurts to read'
**Stephen Laughton**, playwright and screenwriter

'Joyous and heart-wrenching, tender and true, this novel spoke to
and healed something inside me. Danny and Luis have my heart'
**Jeremy Lachlan**, author of the Jane Doe Chronicles

*Also by Tom Rob Smith*

Child 44
The Secret Speech
Agent 6

The Farm

London Spy

Cold People

# Twenty Years Together

## Tom Rob Smith

SIMON & SCHUSTER

London · New York · Amsterdam/Antwerp · Sydney/Melbourne · Toronto · New Delhi

First published in Great Britain by Simon & Schuster UK Ltd, 2026



1 3 5 7 9 10 8 6 4 2

Simon & Schuster UK Ltd, 1st Floor
222 Gray's Inn Road, London WC1X 8HB



Simon & Schuster Australia, Sydney
Simon & Schuster India, New Delhi

www.simonandschuster.co.uk
www.simonandschuster.com.au
www.simonandschuster.co.in

The authorised representative in the EEA is Simon & Schuster Netherlands BV,
Herculesplein 96, 3584 AA Utrecht, Netherlands. info@simonandschuster.nl

Simon & Schuster strongly believes in freedom of expression and stands against
censorship in all its forms. For more information, visit BooksBelong.com

A CIP catalogue record for this book is available from the British Library

Hardback ISBN: 978-1-4711-3314-5
Trade Paperback ISBN: 978-1-4711-3315-2
eBook ISBN: 978-1-4711-3317-6



Typeset in Bembo by M Rules

Printed and Bound in the UK using 100% Renewable Electricity at CPI Group (UK) Ltd

To Panagiotis

# Prologue

## London 1992

## *Living Alone*

After years of sharing digs, Danny Smith had finally found a room of his own. Previously he made do in a basement studio with strangers and single beds separated by paper-partition screens through which he could hear every snore. After the council shut it down as illegal, he couch-surfed for a time, including one weekend where, after refusing to trade sex for a roof over his head, he ended up on a bench in Victoria Embankment Gardens, peering up at the Savoy Hotel. With the help of friends, he secured the smallest bedroom of a flat in Stockwell and to celebrate he visited a garden centre buying damaged plants at a steep discount, the unwanted ones with bent stalks and crushed leaves, convinced he could bring them back to life, the most promising of which now lined his window ledge.

The man standing in Danny's doorway, wearing only socks and a slip, reminded him of these unwanted plants in need of water, affection and sunlight. He was a flatmate's hook-up. They had met at a weekend warehouse rave and had been partying ever since. Danny was about to settle down for an evening of diligent study when the man reappeared looking as lost as it was possible for a grown man to look. The flatmate had left him behind while on a mission to buy supplies. Though the abandoned man could barely speak, no longer sure where he was or what he was doing, he knew that he no longer wanted to be alone.

After loaning the man a pair of tracksuit trousers and a hooded top Danny ventured, 'Here's an idea. Don't wait for Mark to come back. What's going to happen? You carry on for another day? I can give you a sleeping pill and a vitamin pill. You can go home and rest.'

Concerned that the man might still live with his parents or didn't have a home to go to, Danny double-checked, 'Can you go home?'

The man nodded, on the verge of tears.

Danny said, 'Please don't cry. You'll make me cry.'

Danny fetched a Nytol and a multivitamin, carefully wrapping them in a tissue and placing them in the man's hand.

'Let's find your things.'

The bedroom resembled a crime scene. The curtains were wrenched shut. The carpet was littered with improvised ashtrays. The air stank of good times turned stale. Danny found the man's shoes, two upturned trainers among take-out detritus. He deposited the man's shirt and trousers in a plastic bag, salvaging his wallet and keys. As Danny was tying the stranger's laces, the third flatmate returned home from work, warning that Mark would fly into a rage if he came back to find his hook-up missing. Conflict-averse, Danny decided to leave too. He fetched his study material, packing a small rucksack for the evening.

On the streets of South London the freezing February air brought the stranger back to his senses. Shame seeped into his eyes and it became clear that he couldn't be trusted with the challenge of public transport. At a minicab office Danny handed ten pounds to a driver. With the man safely in the back of a cab, he asked how he could pay Danny back. Maybe he meant it literally, the ten pounds. Maybe he meant it a broader sense, this act of kindness. Either way, Danny gave him a hug and told him, 'People helped me.'

After watching the cab drive off Danny opted to walk into Soho rather than catch the tube, partly to save on the fare but also because he kept fit by walking everywhere, harbouring a dislike of gyms dating back to his schooldays where locker rooms were a place of ritual humiliation. Taking his Walkman from his rucksack he put on the head-phones, listening to Freddie Mercury's solo album, *Mr Bad Guy*. Danny's favourite track was 'Living on My Own'. He must have played the song a hundred times, even if it did cut a little close to the bone, or perhaps because it cut so close.

Arriving at Greek Street, Danny found that Soho was subdued, the bars were quiet, the jazz revues were closed and many of the famous theatres were shuttered by the recession. A few hardy souls sat outside the Italian coffee bars, wrapped up in thick coats, smoking like wannabe Cold War spies. Having browsed the pubs Danny spotted a free table at the back of Village Bar. Ordinarily the venue would be busy but tonight, on a Wednesday and in the middle of winter, there was enough life that he wouldn't feel lonely but not so much that he couldn't study. Village Bar had opened the year before, breaking with the legacy of gay venues that shielded the identity of their patrons with blacked-out windows and secluded locations. Village stood at the junction of Old Compton and Wardour Street with bright lights and clear windows, showing off its occupants rather than sheltering them.

Inside Danny ordered an Irish coffee mixed with whiskey, demerara sugar and topped with whipped cream – caffeine, alcohol and dinner all in one. Bringing it back to his table he opened his books, hoping for no more interruptions unless that interruption was a handsome stranger. An hour before closing, Danny made a call to his flat from the payphone at the back of the bar. He heard the news that Mark had returned with another guy, making no reference to the fact that his previous hook-up had been rescued. It was safe to come home. Danny said, 'That's great.'

Except suddenly he didn't feel great. He was about to

reach the milestone of twenty-five years old – a quarter of a century. Danny had never told another man that he loved him. And he had never been told that he was loved.

Danny was about to pack up his books and head home when a man entered the bar, wearing a tailored grey suit and a cashmere scarf, looking like an investment banker who had wandered into the wrong establishment. At a guess the man was in his late twenties. Statuesque and stoic, with broad shoulders and coal-black hair, he attracted plenty of atten-tion. He took a spot at the bar and ordered a bottle of beer. Danny assessed his own clothes. Dressed for warmth and comfort, he was wearing Topman jeans, two pairs of coarse wool socks, a thermal undershirt and a buttercup-yellow hoodie. He didn't stand a chance.

Holding off packing away his books Danny idled at his table watching as various guys made various moves on the well-dressed newcomer, each politely rebuffed. On most days Danny lacked the confidence to approach a stranger sober. But tonight he accepted that he needed to stop hoping for the universe to arrange charming accidental encounters. They were a fantasy. It was time to take matters into his own hands. And hadn't he done a good deed this evening? A stranger for a stranger. Danny's thoughts were often like this – shot through with spurious reasoning. But what was there to lose? If it didn't work out, he was leaving anyway

and he calculated the humiliation would be short lived —
fading by the time he hit the street.

With no basis for believing he might succeed where the
other guys had failed Danny walked to the bar under the
pretext of a drink order he couldn't afford. Standing beside
the man he noticed an earthy cologne, the expensive blends
made from crushed seed pods and natural oils. While waiting for his second Irish coffee to be mixed and before he lost
his nerve, Danny blurted out, 'Who are you waiting for?'

The handsome man turned to him. His eyes were forest
green. Danny had been convinced they would be brown.

'I'm not waiting for anyone.'

It was the slimmest of openings and trying not to fumble
the opportunity, Danny replied, 'I'm not waiting for anyone either.'

Though the line wasn't bad, the timing of his Irish coffee
was lousy. The overzealous bartender had decorated it with
spirals of squirty cream so that it looked like a kid's ice-
cream sundae. Danny was convinced that the immaturity of
his drink would snuff out this fragile connection. He should
have ordered one of those amber spirits served on the rocks
that men in suits sip while smoking cigars. Except this guy
didn't make fun of him. In fact, it was hard to imagine him
making fun of anyone, he was so proper and polite. Danny
suggested, 'How about we not wait for anyone together?'

*

Seated at Danny's table they introduced themselves.

'I'm Luis.'

Sensing that the question was lurking Luis explained that he was Spanish, born in a small city Danny probably had never heard of.

'Try me.'

'Cádiz.'

Danny hadn't heard of it. It was in the south of the country, Luis said, on the coast, a historic trading hub with whitewashed houses, ancient fortifications and a cathedral. Danny pointed out that he too was from a small town on the coast, also one Luis had probably never heard of.

'Try me.'

'Bude.'

Luis hadn't heard of it. It was a pretty town with beautiful beaches, sand dunes, no cathedrals but some cute churches. Glancing at Danny's textbooks Luis asked, 'What are you studying?'

Danny showed him the books.

'I'm training to be a nurse, in a bar, which I know is weird. But the libraries are closed and my home was crazy tonight.'

Flicking through the pages, Luis said that nursing was a great profession. Judging from his tone he sounded sincere. This was important to Danny because lots of people looked down on guys being nurses, wondering why they wouldn't want to be a doctor or a psychiatrist or something more prestigious, by which they often meant more male. After years of dead-end jobs Danny had decided to change direction. He had read in a self-help book that happiness was all about connections, personal and societal. Since he was not a guy with a deep reservoir of self-esteem he hoped this career, while modest in terms of pay, would bolster him in other ways and one day he would become one of those nurses who would hold a patient's hand no matter who they were or how sick they might be.

Luis didn't have much to say about his work other than he was a lawyer. Danny guessed, 'You came here from work?'

Luis nodded and without stopping to consider, Danny followed with, 'You're not out? Are you? I mean – to them?'

Surprised by the directness, Luis shook his head.

'No.'

Changing the subject, Danny admitted, 'I talk too much.'

Luis ventured, 'I don't talk enough.'

Danny said, 'Would you like another beer?'

Danny couldn't afford any more drinks since he had no cash left. But he had his bank card and an interest-free student overdraft and Luis was worth it.

'Isn't this bar closing soon?'

Danny's face fell at the inevitable rejection he had been waiting for. Luis added, 'We could have a drink at my place.'

*

Outside Luis flagged down a black cab, an unaffordable luxury for Danny who fell silent contemplating the cost of the night. A minicab, a black cab and two Irish coffees. But Luis wouldn't hear of splitting the fare, explaining that he would have caught the cab home anyway. He lived alone in a rented apartment on the top floor of an old biscuit factory in East London that had escaped the bombing during the Blitz. In contrast to Danny's room Luis's apartment enjoyed sweeping views stretching from St Paul's Cathedral to the BT Tower. The interior was so spacious that it was easy to imagine big whirring biscuit machines where there was now a sleek Japanese-style low bed. Instead of a wardrobe there was a stainless-steel clothes rail lined with Luis's immaculate suits. Luis apologized for the apartment being so cold.

'It was summer when I rented the place.'

There was not a single plant or item of decoration, no photos or pictures, no personalization of any kind. Everything was functional except for an antique silver necklace, with a small crucifix, on the bedside table beside the books he was reading about Winston Churchill. Catching Danny's curiosity, Luis explained that the books were so he could share the same references as his colleagues. Danny asked, 'Are you good at fitting in?'

Becoming accustomed to the weird questions, Luis replied with a smile.

*

In the kitchen Danny assessed the limited beverage options. There were bottles of Spanish red wine and Scottish whisky. He checked the fridge and found two lemons and a jar of honey in the larder. He asked Luis, 'Have you heard of a drink called a hot toddy?'

Luis shook his head, repeating the odd-sounding name and asking what it was.

'It's Scottish, I think. Or maybe it's Irish. Anyway, it's hot water, lemon, honey and whisky. It's the perfect winter drink.'

Luis seemed concerned.

'Is this apartment so cold?'

Danny shook his head.

'They're fun to make.'

Clattering around in the kitchen Danny produced two hot toddies, strong, not too sweet and decorated with a slice of lemon. And he was right, they were fun to make. Tasting one for the first time, Luis said he liked it very much and they took the drinks into the living room where they stood side by side at the windows looking out over the view. Danny pointed at the spotlit dome of St Paul's and for the sake of saying something declared, 'My favourite building in the world. But I haven't travelled much.'

Danny suddenly felt small. Covering his insecurities he said, 'Have you been to the top?'

Luis shook his head.

'I didn't know you could.'

Speaking without thinking, Danny suggested, 'We should go.'

Too late he realized his mistake, revealing how keen he was. Cool and aloof were the only ways to play it. This was why he was perennially single, he scolded himself, hastening the conversation on.

'I always wondered why they've never filmed an action scene there. A Hitchcock finale. With the villain sliding down the dome to his death.'

Danny finished his drink, still kicking himself for suggesting that they could go on a second date. But before he could say anything else Luis took the glass from Danny's hand, placed it on the floor and kissed him.

Afterwards they lay together in the bed holding each other tightly because the apartment really was very cold. The sex had been good. Luis was in great shape, gym fit and by every traditional definition a heartthrob. When Luis excused himself to go to the bathroom Danny wondered if that was his cue to leave. He decided to take a chance and stay exactly where he was. Minutes later Luis returned, slipping back into the bed and putting his arms around Danny. It was so simple and lovely Danny almost cried. Luis asked, 'Anything you need?'

*Just this*, Danny thought.

*

Luis was a deep sleeper. He didn't move and he didn't make a sound, an ideal partner in bed, Danny concluded. Maybe his body was a little warm but it was a freezing night so that was great for winter. It might be an issue in the summer, Danny continued before smiling at his own stupidity, imagining a summer together before there had even been a tomorrow. He was enjoying the night too much to waste it on sleep but eventually he must have nodded off because when he opened his eyes he saw the night sky turning a bruised shade of blue. Very carefully he lifted Luis's arm and sneaked out of bed, collecting the glasses from the floor and heading into the kitchen where he washed up and wiped down the surfaces. He tidied away the honey, the spoons and the saucepan he had used to heat the water and whisky. He cleaned until the kitchen was spotless. As he was finishing Luis walked in.

'You didn't need to do that.'

Danny shrugged.

'I didn't want to leave a mess.'

That wasn't how he wanted to be remembered, by a sticky spoon and the remains of a squeezed lemon. Luis fell silent and Danny knew he was weighing up whether to suggest that they should meet again. Why would he? Danny wondered. A man as handsome and successful as Luis could walk into any bar and find someone exciting and new. Danny wasn't going to get down about it. If Luis didn't want a second date Danny would be grateful for their perfect night together. He had already devised a solution to avoid any awkwardness.

'I've written down my phone number, so you have it. In case you want to call. No pressure. Up to you. And it doesn't have to be at the top of St Paul's. It could be in a pub. Or a park.'

A park? What was he talking about? Luis picked up the slip of paper, looking at the number. He didn't offer his own. *There's your answer*, Danny thought. He left the kitchen, fetching his clothes and changing quickly.

Danny was ready to leave when Luis joined him.

'This might sound odd.'

Danny tried to reassure him, 'Odd is fine.'

For the first time since they had met, Luis became bashful.

'Would you like to go to a wedding with me?'

The entire evening Luis had been so composed – sane and steady. Then, at six in the morning, he had invited Danny to a wedding. It was even more crazy than suggesting a second date to the top of St Paul's Cathedral. Danny was delighted.

'Sure, Luis. I'd love to go to a wedding with you.'

As an afterthought Danny added, 'Who's getting married?'

*Twenty Years Later*

London 2012

Part One

# Summer

# Chapter One

## *The Wedding Anniversary*

Danny had decided to wear fancy dress, despite worrying that he looked ridiculous. Earlier in the week the outfit seemed fun, playfully interpreting the invitation's theme of 'Summer Love' by dressing up as a lawn tennis player from the 1920s, including flannel trousers, a piqué polo shirt and a knitted V-neck vest. He had found the items in a vintage store on Berwick Street, chancing across a wooden-framed Slazenger racket with fraying strings which now rested on his knees as if between sets. As a gift he had baked a coconut cake with rum-soaked sponge, layers of cream cheese and decorated with marzipan roses, noting, as it neared completion, that it resembled a wedding cake in miniature, which was appropriate since he had made it to celebrate Emma and John's twentieth wedding anniversary – the reason for today's garden party.

With the cake on a porcelain stand under a glass cloche, Danny sat alone on a cedar gazebo under an oak tree in Pembridge Square in Notting Hill. Protected by a high privet hedge he was hidden from the other guests arriving at the house. Strictly speaking he was trespassing – this was one of London's exclusive gardens for residents only, enclosed by a wrought-iron fence and requiring a key to access it. He had slipped in as an older woman entered on her early-evening stroll, catching the gate before it closed. She had assessed him, sceptical that he was a resident of such a prestigious address. However, observing the coconut cake and tennis attire, she had refrained from saying anything. After all, how dangerous could such a man be? Once inside the square Danny toured the flower beds before discovering the gazebo where he now sat, waiting for Luis to show up and save him from the embarrassment of making an entrance to this high society garden party on his own, knowing almost no one and most likely the only man in fancy dress.

Even though it was a Saturday Luis was working. He was now at the prestigious Allen & Overy, one of London's top law firms. He often worked late and occasionally at week-ends, intent on becoming a partner by the age of fifty. So far Danny had already spent an hour waiting in a Turkish coffee shop near Notting Hill Gate tube station, sipping an iced cardamom coffee and reading various newspapers' gloomy predictions about the upcoming London Olympics. Grown restless with caffeine and pessimism, Danny had sent Luis a text message as a gentle nudge, saying that the frosting on his cake was starting to slip and he couldn't wait any longer. He was heading to the party, hoping to jolt a reply. But as he approached the white stucco house on the corner, more embassy than family home, he lost his nerve, continuing past the front door, orbiting the square until he seized his chance to sneak into the private gardens.

None of this explained why Danny was feeling sad. He wasn't upset that Luis was late, the cake wasn't ruined, and he was in no rush to join the party. To cheer himself up he decided to vape. After quitting smoking, Danny became an early adopter of vaping. Today's selection was Sunshine Watermelon, an appropriate antidote to a bout of the summertime blues. Carefully refilling the device, Danny took a hit and exhaled a plume of fruity vapour. Barely a minute later the woman appeared by his side. If the cake had won him a sliver of credibility the vape cost him every shred of it.

'You're not a resident, are you?'

He shook his head.

'No. I'm going to Emma and John's wedding anniversary. They're throwing a garden party. They live on this square.'

At the mention of their names, her tone recalibrated.

'A wonderful couple. But they're not hosting the party here. They have a garden of their own.'

He knew this, of course.

'I'm waiting for my partner to arrive.'

The woman suggested, 'Wouldn't it be better if she met you at the party?'

Danny took another hit on his vape, exhaling and wondering if he should bother to correct the mistake.

'My partner is a man.'

She nodded, as if with that admission his clothes, his cake and his failure to understand the rules of this place now made sense.

'Let me show you to the house.'

Danny stood up and followed her to the gate. No doubt this woman, the Sheriff of Pembridge Square, would watch him until the moment he rang the doorbell. Holding the tennis racket in one hand and the cake stand in the other, he climbed the stone steps to the front door, accepting that he would now have to enter the party by himself.

Opening the door Emma said his name as though there were no one else in the world she would rather see, before asking, 'Where's Luis?'

Danny attended these parties by way of a guest pass rather than full membership. If you wanted Luis, the deal was some guy called Danny would tag along. He explained that Luis was running late. Emma expressed her admiration that Danny had come alone.

'I didn't want to miss the speeches.'

She placed her hand on his arm, letting him into a secret.

'I have no idea what I'm going to say.'

'You always know what to say.'

Perhaps it was an inappropriate observation, too direct and personal, but Danny often misjudged conversational cues. Emma reminded herself of precisely that fact before changing the subject.

'You baked this?'

Bashful, he nodded.

'The stand is for you as well.'

It was Wedgwood china with an herbarium print found in a Bermondsey flea market, priced at five pounds, bought for five pounds. Danny hated to haggle.

'I read somewhere that you're supposed to give a gift of china on a twentieth wedding anniversary.'

Emma seemed impressed, claiming that Danny knew far more about wedding anniversaries than she did. Accepting the stand, she studied the cake under the cloche.

'I see roses, but I smell watermelon?'

Danny made a mental note never to vape around his cakes again.

'You don't have to serve it.'

Emma dismissed the suggestion.

'You're the only person who bothered to make us something.'

Emma's father had been the British ambassador to Nepal,

and she had grown up mingling with dignitaries and politicians, cultivating an effortless manner around people of power. Partly for this reason Danny always felt childish around her – she was so profoundly adult, not merely in terms of age. She was forty-nine, only four years older than him. Yet their lives were solar systems apart. As they walked through her family house she discreetly inspected his outfit.

Danny asked, 'Is it too much?'

She shook her head.

'You look dashing – like the tennis coach in a country mansion murder mystery.'

Danny imagined the character, not the owner of the estate but the man teaching the aristocrats. By contrast Emma's clothes captured the essence of summer joy without being anything as tacky as a costume, such as this dress by Alice Temperley, the pattern so vivid it was as though real meadow flowers had been snatched from the field and stitched directly onto the fabric.

'Please tell me I'm not the only one in fancy dress?'

Ducking the question she said, 'Let's fix you a drink.'

They entered a glass conservatory with the doors thrown open, leading to a stone-walled garden where some fifty guests were gathered, their children playing on a padded plaid blanket spread on the lawn. At the back of the garden evening sunlight broke through the branches of a chestnut tree. An unseen neighbour was hosting a barbecue, their grill throwing up wisps of charcoal smoke which, at most parties, would have been an irritation but tonight swirled above the heads of the guests, catching the rays of sun as if there was nothing in this world which couldn't be corralled to Emma's advantage.

A buffet was spread across several tables, bowls of green pea salad, plates of buttered asparagus and a whole poached salmon. There were pitchers of summer punch with cubes of melon and sprigs of fresh mint. If it wasn't for the presence of waiters in crisp white shirts and beige canvas aprons circulating with champagne it would have been difficult to guess that the party had been catered. Emma set Danny's cake on the dessert table among bowls of quartered strawberries. As he feared, the frosting had slipped, losing some of its firmness. Noticing his disappointment Emma picked up a serving knife and extracted the disfigured portion of the cake, a small but perfectly formed act of kindness.

'Why don't you help yourself and head outside?'

With that, Danny was on his own.

Deciding against taking any food he toyed with the idea of abandoning the tennis racket. In the end he kept it. Without the prop people might wonder if these were his regular clothes. He stepped into the garden, racket in one hand, a glass of punch in the other. The men were dressed in cotton suits with blue shirts, a few with Panama hats trimmed with a traditional grosgrain ribbon. The women were wearing white dresses with oversized belts – a collection of clothes curated for a summer catalogue.

Unable to spy an inroad to any of the conversations, Danny found himself at the end of the garden examining the vegetable patch and herb garden. Sipping the punch, a blend of spiced rum, pineapple pulp and fresh ginger, he crouched down to attend to the rosemary as though he were the genial gardener who had been asked to join the party and didn't feel comfortable talking to the other guests. It was at this point that he heard his name being called and turned to see John approaching, guessing that Emma had dispatched her husband to interrupt his self-imposed exile. They shook hands with the grip of men concluding negotiations for an oilfield deal and Danny congratulated him on twenty years of marriage.

'Thank you, yes, hard to believe. I've no idea where the time has gone.'

Danny thought about the townhouse, the garden, the three children, the lauded career and the country cottage in the Cotswolds. Instead, he observed, 'You know that Luis and me—'

He corrected himself.

'Luis and I, we've been together for twenty years.'

John adjusted his tortoiseshell glasses, considering this fact as if not entirely sure of it.

'We *have* known you two for a long time.'

*More than that*, Danny thought.

'Luis brought me to your wedding.'

Belatedly warming to the subject, John nodded. 'Yes, that's right. I remember now. Three years I'd worked with the fellow and no one in the office had a clue about his personal life. He was a handsome Spanish enigma. When we invited him to the wedding, we insisted that he bring a guest. To flush him out. We all wondered what kind of girl he'd bring.'

Luis's invitation to Danny had been his way of coming out to his colleagues.

'I'm his kind of girl.'

John laughed uncertainly.

'Yes, I suppose you are. None of us had guessed that he was gay. You broke a lot of girls' hearts, I can tell you.'

Sensing that he'd said something clumsy he hastily added, 'Anyway, twenty years, huh?'

Danny reformulated the point.

'For as long as you've been married.'

John mused, 'It was on off for a while, wasn't it?'

'No.'

'No?'

'No.'

'Well, here's to *your* twenty years.'

Danny worried that he was forcing an inappropriate parallel between their relationships, an imposter crassly elbowing his way into someone's celebrations. After their glasses clinked, they both fell silent, saved only by the arrival of Luis.

# Chapter Two

## *Speeches*

While Emma introduced Luis to several important guests his eyes sought out Danny, giving him an apologetic smile, able to imagine the awkward exchanges he had missed. Luis hadn't fussed with the dress code, merely unbuttoning his collar and taking off his tie. Yet he still managed to be the best dressed-man at the party, wearing Burberry cotton trousers, shot through with silk which gave them a shimmer in the evening sun. Over the years he had maintained a rigorous routine at the gym and his shoulders remained broad while his once coal-black hair was now a salt-and-pepper mix. To many observers Danny and Luis appeared to have little in common. A keen long-distance runner, slim in stature, Danny had a discreet strength whereas Luis looked like he once enjoyed team sports. Luis's thought process was rooted in facts and to the point; he was knowl-edgeable on a wide range of subjects and able to converse in three languages. By contrast Danny's thoughts hopscotched from subject to subject, often sounding jumbled in the only language he knew. What seemed to be an odd couple was eventually reframed, as onlookers assigned them familiar roles – some version of a husband and a wife.

John strode off to greet Luis while Danny stayed put in the herb garden, watching as Emma and John escorted Luis through the social groups that he himself had drifted past without a word. Luis, as a man, was recognizable to these people as one of their own, distinguished, professional, successful, with a sturdy Swiss wristwatch. After spending an acceptable amount of time mingling Luis took leave of the conversations and arrived at Danny's side where they stood for a moment, unsure whether a kiss might be a spectacle. At a private party like this people would notice but probably no one would care. However, caution had so muddied their minds that it required a conscious effort to push any concerns aside. In the end, Danny kissed Luis on the lips with as much propriety as if he were placing a full stop at the end of a sentence. Luis, in response, took hold of the frayed-string racket, spinning it in his hands.

Danny observed, 'No one else has dressed up.'

Luis glanced at the other guests.

'But you knew this before you arrived, no? You wanted to turn up and play the odd one out.'

Danny considered the idea.

'I've never needed to play at being the outsider.'

Standing on the steps to the conservatory Emma clinked a knife against a glass, signalling that the moment had arrived for speeches. Parents gathered their children as the waiters topped up champagne flutes in preparation for a toast. Keen to hear every word Danny and Luis took up positions close to the front. Danny had always loved speeches, not political or professional speeches but ceremonial ones at birthdays, weddings or anniversaries. Witty or drunken, he loved them all, but his favourite kind were emotional speeches where lips trembled and words faltered.

John spoke first. Even though he was a partner at one of the most ruthlessly adversarial London law firms, his manner outside of court was that of an absent-minded academic, able to afford this bumbling, bespectacled English gentleman routine because there was never any question of him not being taken seriously.

'When I asked Emma to marry me, I was sure that the answer would be no. My destiny, I believed, was to be the man she dated while she figured out what she did and didn't want from a relationship. The truth is that she should have said no. I wasn't ready for her. I wasn't good enough, not even close. Instead of ditching me to find the man she was looking for, she gave me the chance to become the man she was looking for and a husband worthy of her. She taught me everything that is important in life. Here we are, all these years later, with our beautiful children and our dearest friends. I'm forever grateful to Emma for seeing in me someone I didn't know I could be.'

Moved by the tenderness of his words Emma took a beat to collect herself before joking, 'I knew I should've gone first.'

After the laughter subsided she began, 'It has been brought to my attention that I can seem annoyingly happy most of the time, infuriatingly optimistic and irritatingly upbeat. But when I met John, I was lost. I'd been hurt and hurt again and I was one heartbreak away from becoming jaded. John taught me that love could be healing, that it didn't involve anger or manipulation. He showed me that love can lift you up, it can make you tall and it can be straightforward without any agenda other than our mutual happiness. He is the best husband and father a woman could wish for.'

The guests raised their glasses saying 'to John and Emma' or 'to Emma and John'. Danny also raised his glass, unable to join in the chorus of toasts because he was crying. Luis turned to him, observing his tears. On the cusp of asking what was wrong, Luis caught himself. A sentimental soul, who often cried, tears from Danny needed no explanation. Except as the guests broke apart Danny wanted to explain – but Luis was already congratulating the married couple.

Chapter Three


*What Are We Talking About?*


By the end of the party Danny was drunk on rum punch having eaten nothing more than mint leaves and melon cubes. As the sky grew dark the party became a more adult affair. Waiters lit candles inside silk lanterns that hung from the conservatory to the chestnut tree. Those staying late sat on oversize Marrakech-made cushions around a log-burning fire pit. Danny shared a cushion with Luis, even though there were plenty to spare, making a show of the fact that they were the only gay couple at this party. Someone asked how they met. Danny wondered why of all the couples here only they were being asked this question, as if their love story were all beginning and no middle. Luis replied, 'We're pre-internet and pre-apps. We met the old-fashioned way, face to face in a bar.'

When they finally said goodbye Danny told Emma and John that their anniversary was as perfect as their wedding, a winter ceremony that took place in the great hall of a stately manor under a floral arch of delphiniums, cow parsley and lupins with a foot of snow outside. Because Emma's father had been terminally ill, they had brought the wedding forward to ensure that he could attend. His short speech, in a rasping voice, moved everyone to tears. Recalling these details Danny wondered why they hadn't also celebrated their anniversary in the winter. Emma replied that it didn't matter when you celebrate so long as you celebrate. Danny marvelled at this wisdom. John gave him a pat on the back while Emma kissed him on the cheek, calling him adorable and congratulating him on every crumb of his coconut cake being eaten. He'd congratulated their anniversary. They'd congratulated his baking.

Uncharacteristically quiet in the cab home Danny cracked open the window to allow in a breeze. He said, 'It didn't bother you? The way they spoke about our relationship?'

Luis was confused by the question.

'How did they speak about us?'

Danny took a moment to find the right word.

'It wasn't belittling?'

Luis shook his head.

'It didn't feel that way to me.'

Danny had the ability to feel fifty things at once and he often checked in with Luis for a read. Meanwhile, Luis depended on Danny for a sensitivity to emotional undercurrents, often underestimating the value of gestures such as baking a cake rather than buying one. With a steadying hand on Danny's knee, Luis said, 'We're almost home.'

Home was a one-bedroom attic apartment in Kennington – a Georgian townhouse divided into apartments in the 1960s, with the top floor enjoying sloping skylights, uneven wood floors and a balcony with views towards the housing estates of Elephant and Castle. Climbing the narrow flight of communal stairs, Danny dropped his keys before reaching their front door.

'Do you love me?'

Luis laughed.

'Very much.'

But Danny wasn't done.

'You don't need me to be more . . .'

Maybe he didn't mean *more* at all. Maybe the word he was looking for was *less*. Luis kissed him on the cheek and opened the door.

While Luis showered Danny stripped down to his pistachio-coloured briefs, leaving his vintage tennis attire heaped on the couch. He had no idea where his Slazenger racket was – lost in the herb garden somewhere. Even though it was past midnight he filled his steel watering can and began tending to the lavender, jasmine and honeysuckle so densely arranged on their balcony that there was barely enough space to stand. The plants in their terracotta pots were glad for a drink after the heat of the day. Finished, he set down the watering can and leaned on the rail, following the progress of a lithe black cat walking atop a fence. Having taken the balcony as far as it could go, Danny imagined owning a garden and tending to rows of marrows and squashes. He pictured a crumbling stone wall for climbing vines, a cedarwood gazebo coiled with wisteria where he could read and vape.

He and Luis had bought this apartment early on in their relationship. The property had been a wreck, a studio attic belonging to an aspiring artist who had left the interior with paint-flecked walls and populated with pinboards of nude male Polaroids. In despair, the artist had taken his own life, a tragedy which resulted in the apartment being sold on the cheap by relatives too disgusted with their kin to inspect the property, let alone clean it up. Luis had resisted buying it, his Catholic spirituality unnerved by the death, but Danny wanted to reverse the sadness of this space, arguing that they would never get a better chance at owning their own home. They pooled their savings and applied for a joint mortgage which at that time required HIV tests, a demand Danny queried. Declined by every major lender they eventually found a brokerage firm which assisted gay buyers navigate a hostile financial world.

In retrospect buying a place together had taken on the significance of a proxy commitment ceremony. It wasn't as fun; there had been no party, no vows, no dressing-up, no marquees and no floral arch, but there were documents to sign, and in the absence of a wedding it served as a legal expression of their devotion to each other. Luis pointed out that gay couples had been using property law for many hundreds of years as the only way of solemnizing their union, referencing Spanish academics who found deeds in the Monastery of Celanova, in Galicia, which recorded the property purchase by Pedro Díaz and Muño Vandilaz. The document made it clear that the two men shared their lives as well as their home – arguably the first recorded gay union in history, dating back over nine hundred years to 1061. Property as promise. A title deed for a ring.

Emerging from the shower with a towel around his waist, Luis mixed an Old Fashioned using Macallan whisky, sculpting a coil of orange peel – a man who rarely did anything unless he could do it well. Looking towards the open balcony doors he asked if Danny wanted a drink.

'I want a garden.'

Luis replied, 'All I can offer right now is a drink.'

Danny stood firm.

'What are we waiting for?'

Taking a sip of his Old Fashioned, Luis pointed out, 'I didn't realize we were waiting for anything.'

Guessing the inspiration for Danny's desire, Luis added, 'A garden in Notting Hill is out of our reach.'

Danny shook his head.

'I don't want their garden. I want our garden. I want to know what our garden would be. Wasn't the best part about owning this apartment making it ours? Taking something rundown and fixing it up. I want to do that again. This time with a garden.'

Luis put down his drink.

'A garden you've never mentioned before?'

Danny shot back, 'I never realized how much I wanted one before.'

Bringing the conversation to an end, Luis asked, 'Can we have sex and talk about it tomorrow?'

Danny weighed the proposition seriously before declaring, 'Sure.'

# Chapter Four

## *Water Is a Cure*

On Sunday morning Danny woke with a hangover, convinced that he had made a fool out of himself at the garden party. That his role was either clown or carer. Wrapping himself in a blanket he sat on the balcony, his bare feet nestled among the plant pots, dozing in the sun. His intermittent dreams incorporated a miscellany of summer sounds including music from an ice-cream van and the laughter of children playing in the nearby park. After a time, he went inside where Luis was reading the international print editions of *El País* and *El Mundo*, a fixture of his weekends. Danny lay on the sofa, resting his head on Luis's legs, listening to the crinkle of the pages.

*

Danny decided to shake off his malaise by swimming at the Hampstead Ponds. He was a regular at the Men's Ponds ever since he moved to London from Bude. Water was a big part of Danny's childhood. In the summer months he would swim in the sea, enjoying the sensation of being underwater, his fingertips brushing the seabed, holding his breath for as long as possible, sheltering from the world above. As a teenager he read obsessively about mermaids and mermen, from the historical accounts of explorers who spotted them at a galleon's bow to their fictional incarnations, longing for an invitation to join their underwater society.

In search of a replacement for the sea, Danny discovered the Ponds. Over time he developed an appreciation of them as a place in London like no other. Some swimmers showed up for the exercise, the Orthodox Jews and fitness fanatics, others for fun, boisterous groups of straight friends intermingling with gay guys who turned up to talk, hang out, hook up, sunbathe nude and generally treat the Ponds as an outdoor social club, spending hours with a book or embroiled in conversation. It was a space free from indicators of money or status, with everyone sitting on their small patch of sun-baked concrete swapping stories over handfuls of berries.

Unofficial chairman of this social club was Chris, a retired civil servant in his early seventies, a man with an encyclopaedic mind who had devoted his professional life to the service of his country and who now spent his summers by the Ponds and his winters by the fire. As lean as a competitive swimmer with a deep tan, cropped silver hair and a silver beard, his appearance resembled a handsome desert-island castaway who, despite being stranded, somehow managed to keep up appearances. He wore sapphire blue Speedos with a white trim and sat among an ever-changing court of miscellaneous men discussing anything from travel plans to politics, flipping from the frivolous to the sincere. One enduring topic of discussion was the looming fear that the council would regulate the Ponds, installing ticket barriers and tearing down the nude sunbathing area, forcing them into well-behaved conformity with every other humdrum municipal swimming pool across town. Out of habit Danny would sit within Chris's orbit, answering questions but posing few of his own, acknowledging his position as a junior member of this queer social club.

Today was different. During three brisk laps, circling beneath red kites and grey herons, Danny plucked up the courage to ask Chris a personal question, breaking an unwritten rule that intimate information should be volunteered and never solicited.

'Was there ever someone?'

Putting aside his book Chris scrutinized Danny, trying to figure out whether he should make a joke or answer honestly.

'Someone special? Yes. A long time ago. He was a teacher. One of those inspirational types. Thought he could make the world a better place. We were together for two years. The best years of my life. He wanted to move in with me. And I said no.'

Chris studied Danny's face.

'You can't imagine it, can you? Saying no to a man you love?'

Danny couldn't imagine it. He would do anything for Luis. And he was sure Luis would do anything for him. Chris continued, 'I was working in the Foreign Office at the time. The Sexual Offences Act was the law. If they found out that I was living with a man, it would've been the end of my career. And I was ambitious so I kept him on the side. But being on the side wasn't enough for him. He was fearless. I was not. By the time I realized what a terrible mistake I'd made, he was sick. The only place he could survive was in a hospital. When I shared my regrets, I saw disdain in his eyes – that it was easy for me to offer my home now that it was impossible for him to accept.'

Almost talking to himself, Chris concluded, 'On the side is all I could offer. On the side is all I knew. On the side is all I'll ever know.'

With that he returned to the pages of his book, signalling that the conversation was at an end. Danny packed up his things and rather than catch the tube, decided to walk all the way home, down Primrose Hill and through Regent's Park.

That evening Luis prepared a dinner of buttery scrambled eggs, heaped on slices of toasted sourdough. Out of nowhere, Danny declared, 'What if we sold the apartment and bought a boat and sailed around the world?'

Luis helped himself to more scrambled eggs and talked about the sail boats he used to watch depart from the port of Cádiz. Danny wanted to tell Luis he was being serious except of course he didn't know the first thing about boats despite having grown up on the coast.

Before going to sleep Danny changed the bed linen, a habit of his when he hankered after the psychological sensation of a fresh start. In the shower, quite inexplicably, he wept.

# Chapter Five

## *A Danish Marriage*

Though the weekend shifts could be gruelling, Danny didn't mind being busy that Friday night, hoping it would distract him from his persistent melancholy thoughts – that he was somehow incomplete. Back in his twenties these feelings of incompleteness in part explained why Danny had trained to become a nurse. As a career it had not been his first choice. He had studied theatre at the University of Essex, not acting or directing but the stagecraft, lighting and sound design, arriving in London with dreams of creating fantastical worlds from nothing more than plywood, paint and nails. However, his graduation coincided with a recession and soaring unemployment, one of the worst times to be looking for a job, let alone being a young man with no connections or professional experience. Many West End productions were closing, only the biggest shows survived the downturn, such as *Starlight Express* and *Cats*. Living on bowls of cereal for breakfast and dinner with cups of bitter black coffee to suppress his hunger, Danny hauled himself from theatre to theatre, becoming numb to rejection, his hope dropping close to the minimum threshold required to climb out of bed in the morning.

To make ends meet he found work as an usher at the hit show *Jeffrey Bernard Is Unwell*, playing on Shaftesbury Avenue and starring Peter O'Toole. Earning three pounds an hour, he sold two-pound tubs of Jersey ice cream to some of the most important people in the entertainment business. Rather than living his dream, he was dream-adjacent, figuring that proximity would sustain him until he found a foothold. Night after night he watched the sallow figure of O'Toole ridicule the concept of settling down to an appreciative audience that had, by and large, settled down. Wearing a clip-on bow tie that never stayed straight, berated by customers outraged that the ice-cream queue moved too slowly, Danny wondered whether he was pursuing a true calling in life or whether he was here because, at school, the only gay teacher had run the theatre department. Looking back could his career have been different if his science teacher hadn't mocked his voice, or the sports coach ridiculed his run? It seemed that his life's journey had been shaped by avoiding other people's animosity rather than having any kind of plan, leaving him unable to answer the question of whether he had made his way or whether his way had been made for him.

One evening after work he caught a late-night television interview with Peter O'Toole and presenter Melvyn Bragg. It was a discussion about alcohol, addiction and acting. Midway through, while demonstrating how to hold his drinking glass, Peter O'Toole described Jeffrey Bernard's way of drinking as 'poofy' to laughter from the audience and no admonishment from his host. The next day Danny returned his usher's bow tie – and the dream with it. He began studying for a nursing degree at King's College London, eager to play some part in society in a measurable way. And Danny took pride in being a nurse, able to tolerate the long hours for the belief that he mattered. He had worked at hospitals across the city, ending up at St Thomas' on the South Bank where he had cared for several prominent politicians, some of whom he helped return to health only for them to cross the river and vote against his rights.

For a long time, he had life figured out. He was living with a man he loved, in a place of their own, able to walk to work, often early in the morning, catching the sun rising over the city he had come to call home. Danny had carved himself a groove. He was happy. Fundamentally he was a happy guy, which made this feeling of incompleteness all the harder to comprehend. It wasn't the deafening sadness of his early twenties; it was faint, like the mutterings of a conversation he couldn't quite hear.

Passing the patient discharge lounge Danny noticed an elderly woman struggling with the remote control to the television, her fingers too stiff to operate the buttons. Normally there was a nurse supervising the room, but unable to see anyone on duty he stopped by to help. She explained that she didn't want to watch the news and Danny was about to change channel when the bulletin began a report from Copenhagen where gay marriage had just been made legal. After pioneering the framework of registered partnerships for gay couples back in 1989 Denmark was, after twenty-three years, allowing them to marry. The law had passed the Danish Folketinget on 7 June, was signed by Queen Margrethe II on the 12th and come into effect today – Friday the 15th. Seizing the opportunity a businessman named Stig Elling had married Steen Andersen, his partner of twenty-seven years. When asked by a journalist how they planned to celebrate, Stig answered, 'With champagne and a good dinner.'

Danny was so engrossed in the story of their marriage that he forgot to change the channel. Looking down at the woman, he smiled sheepishly as if caught out, hastily flicking through soap operas and quiz shows. When she told him to go back to the news he said that it wasn't necessary, he'd seen enough. But she insisted. Danny obliged and the two of them watched the footage of Stig and Steen being photographed by the world's press, a modest couple perplexed by the global interest in their love story. The segment concluded, moving on to coverage of the London Olympics. Touching her wedding ring, the woman said, 'I lost my husband last year. We exchanged our vows in Lewisham's register office when I was twenty-four years old, which was considered old back then. It's not the prettiest of places but it did the job. Afterwards we went to the pub. There were twelve of us. We ate cottage pie and apple crumble. I drank a half-pint of Guinness. To this day, I still regret not organizing a proper wedding. We should've celebrated. We should've danced. That wasn't how it was done back then – well, not by people like me. Big weddings were for people with money. But I should've stood firm. It's one of the few days you remember for the rest of your life. Take it from me.'

She concluded, placing her frail hand on top of his, 'There aren't many of those.'

# Chapter Six

## *Five Burning Rings*

In a quirk of fate quitting the theatre business to become a nurse presented Danny with the chance to become involved in the biggest theatrical event in global broadcasting – the Olympic opening ceremony. With under a third of the budget of Beijing's opening ceremony the British production was depending on eccentricity and creativity to make an impression. The request for doctors and nurses to take part took everyone by surprise since no one associated the National Health Service with the Olympic Games. However, the remit was to showcase anything that was great about the host country, and the director, Academy Award-winning Danny Boyle, selected the National Health Service. The ceremony's stage was the purpose-built Stratford stadium in East London, once a neighbourhood of derelict factories and polluted canals. Though some commentators mocked the stadium's utilitarian design compared to the grandeur of Beijing's 'bird's nest' there were hidden triumphs behind its creation, including a massive clean-up operation. Tonnes of arsenic and asbestos were removed from the grounds; decades of dirty coal tar were sieved from the soil. Where there had once been poisons, there was now a park.

Ignoring the naysayers and recalling the excitement of his student theatre days, Danny had put himself forward. Rehearsals started in an abandoned car factory in Dagenham with thousands of dancers and volunteers participating in a process taking many months, with bumps along the way, from government interference to cast replacements and a national crisis of confidence. Yet Danny never lost faith, enjoying every moment, making new friends, including Matt, a mental health nurse from Park Royal Hospital in West London. Finally, the rehearsals moved into the completed stadium. Although Luis couldn't be in the audience on the opening night since tickets were largely set aside for visiting dignitaries, he attended the dress rehearsal and loved the show so much, he organized a viewing party for their friends at the outdoor terrace of Yard Bar in Soho where he would be cheerleading the crowd.

Waiting for the show to start in a holding area situated off the main stage and dressed in a nurse's uniform from 1948, the year the National Health Service was founded, Danny focused his hopes on the overcast sky, the audience and the entire nation in willing the storm clouds to pass. At nine in the evening, on Friday 27 July, the collective prayers seemed to bring the rains to a stop. The stadium started the countdown from ten. The Olympic bronze bell sounded out. With preternatural confidence, one young chorister, a boy of eleven, sang the hymn 'Jerusalem', the unofficial national anthem, to a pin-drop silent auditorium, and the ceremony began.

In the centre of the stadium was a recreation of Glastonbury Tor planted with living grass and meadow flowers, surrounded by fields populated with a cast of wandering farmers herding goats and geese. The actors were dressed in coarse wools and baggy linens, ambling under paper cumulus clouds in a vision that blended the beauty of a John Constable landscape with the absurd-surreal joy of a Monty Python sketch.

With a switch in tempo set to the beat of steel drums the Industrial Revolution was ushered in by a change of cast dressed in tails and top hats, merchants and traders. Leading them was actor Kenneth Branagh playing the part of engineer Isambard Kingdom Brunel, the mind behind architectural marvels such as the Clifton Suspension Bridge and the original Hungerford Suspension Bridge across the Thames.

As with all great shows, it was possible to project your own life experiences onto the events on stage, with Danny recalling the night when he had stood on Hungerford Bridge, staring down into the Thames, at his lowest ebb, homeless, loveless, drunk on cheap gin and wondering if he should jump into the dark waters below. He had been saved by the city skyline – the spotlit dome of St Paul's Cathedral to the north and the illuminations of the National Theatre to the south. Understanding that suicide would be the end of everything, not only the end of sadness but also curiosity, delight, laughter, hopes, dreams and the pursuit of love, he walked off the bridge, telling himself that he couldn't die without experiencing love – no one should die before they've experienced love. He had bought a falafel-stuffed pitta from a food stall on the South Bank, a place he had never found again as if it had magically appeared that night, and sat on the cold stone steps down to the river, his fingers dripping with tahini sauce. In the months afterwards he had enrolled in nursing college, met Luis and turned his life around.

Taking centre stage, Kenneth Branagh performed a fragment from Shakespeare's *The Tempest* – the 'Be not afraid' speech, where the creature Caliban described the magical properties of a wondrous isle seen in an exquisite dream: *When I wak'd, I cried to dream again.* Danny knew this play, having built the sets for a production at university, and these lines had stayed with him – the anguish of waking up from an exquisite dream and longing to return to sleep. As a closeted teenager Danny had dreamed about surviving a shipwreck on a remote Pacific Island with one other man, believing that the only way two men could be in a relationship was if they were marooned with no other people to judge and no laws or society to stand in their way, dreams he preferred to reality. The play seemed to have followed him throughout his life. Sitting in a Soho cinema in 1991 he had watched a film adaptation of *The Tempest* called *Prospero's Books*, directed by Peter Greenaway, spellbound by the naked figure of Caliban played by renowned dancer Michael Clark – magnificent, Danny had thought, the shape of his body and the way this dancer moved. The thought was a revelation, that it wasn't grubby or sordid to admire a man, that men's bodies could be beautiful too.

At the end of Branagh's performance the windmills collapsed, the countryside broke apart, and the towering blast furnaces of northern England pushed up from beneath the stage – chimney stacks bellowing steam while a cast of steeplejacks and labourers pounded the stage with giant hammers. From five forges rose five colossal rings. Molten red. Newly pressed. Lifted from separate segments of the stage, they joined together in the air to form the Olympic symbol. As the five rings touched, their surfaces blazed and curtains of golden sparks fell.

Many in the cast wept for joy as they watched but Danny's elation turned inward, realizing what he should do – what he should have done years ago. This island had given him many opportunities, from performing in an Olympic ceremony, to becoming a nurse, to loving openly and now it was time to take another. Inspired by a national celebration, he was going to create a personal one. He was going to ask Luis to marry him. And he was going to ask him tonight.

Chapter Seven

*How Do You Propose?*

The opening ceremony lasted three hours from the chiming of the bronze bell to the firework finish. In the show's second act Danny took to the stage, managing without a stumble to perform his small role. Nurses, doctors and volunteers danced around illuminated hospital beds, each bed carrying a young child, some of them patients from Great Ormond Street Hospital who might not live long enough to see another Olympic Games. Among his fellow cast members, Danny experienced an emotion he was rarely allowed to feel – a sense of national pride. In the past, when the government passed laws excluding him and newspapers ridiculed the few who were prominent while ignoring the many who were sick, patriotism always seemed a prize for others. But it was his as much as it belonged to anyone, and it felt wonderful right now to be part of a country that had staged such a great party for the whole world.

By the time Danny and his friend Matt cleared the stadium it was one in the morning. Neither of them had eaten anything before the show and since Danny had been abstaining from alcohol in the weeks leading up to the performance the cans of Marks & Spencer premixed gin and slimline tonic that they had stashed to celebrate made them tipsy, high-fiving strangers as they walked to the nearby Underground station which was operating late to transport the crowd home. Danny phoned Luis, arranging to meet him at Matt's afterparty where celebrations were already underway. Over the bar's din Luis declared that it was one of the best nights of his life. The truth was that Luis had been part of every great day in Danny's life, and he wanted him to be part of every great day going forward, which was another way of saying they should get married. Looking back, Danny had been circling the idea for months. The mystery of his sadness was solved. Marriage was missing, a public celebration of their relationship. And yes, it was true, Danny was aware that they weren't technically allowed to *marry*, this wasn't Denmark or Spain or the Netherlands. The law in England still prohibited it. But that was the verb – *to marry* – and okay, so it would be a *civil* ceremony, he and Luis would be *civil partners*, but no one got down on one knee and asked someone to *civil ceremony* with them. The question everyone asked, whether they were allowed to or not, was – will you marry me?

On the crowded tube carriage into central London people were singing and drinking and Danny did something he normally never did with drunk strangers on a tube – he joined in.

Matt lived in a Victorian mansion block near the Royal Vauxhall Tavern, a popular after-hours house. He was single, handsome, thirty-seven years old, in great shape from a routine of early-morning workouts and late-night dancing. But if you knew where to look, and Danny did know, there were lines of loneliness around his eyes. Before they went into the flat Matt suggested they smoke a joint and Danny nodded, aware that after tonight they would drift apart, no matter how hard they tried to stay close. Their shifts were too long and, without the rehearsals to bind them together, they would see each other maybe once or twice a year. He could sense that Matt wanted to make a move, but he admired Danny's relationship with Luis and was yearning for one of his own. A kiss would feel less like affection and more like jealousy and a kiss should create something special rather than damage it. Matt peered up through the pollution at the muted stars and said without a trace of hyperbole, 'That was the best day of my life.'

Having heard this phrase from Luis and now from Matt,

it occurred to Danny that most people described their wedding day in those terms. A day none of them had ever been allowed to enjoy. He shared a few half-hearted drags on the joint, not caring much for weed which made him woozy rather than witty. At the end of the smoke they hugged, holding on to their connection for as long as possible.

Upstairs the party was messy and young. Danny weaved his way through the guests, many of whom were high, none of whom he knew, eventually finding Luis seated in the living room on a shamrock green sofa, nursing a bottle of Modelo beer. Commotion swirled around him while he waited patiently like a lifeguard on a raucous gay beach. The music of Robyn and Rihanna was straining the speakers of the sound system.

Surveying the scene Danny understood that this party was not the place to propose – proposing needed planning, preparation and an attention to detail. He had made the decision tonight but that didn't mean he was required to blurt it out at the first opportunity. Luis might think that Danny was drunk or trying to stretch out the night's happiness, ricocheting from one ceremony to another. He needed Luis to be sure that their rendition of the world's most romantic question had been twenty years in the making.

Approaching the sofa, Danny offered his hand to Luis.

'Let's go home.'

To his surprise Luis rejected the idea. This night was special, one of a kind, and he wanted to make the most of it. Instead of standing up he indicated for Danny to sit beside him, wrapping an arm around him and declaring, 'Watching you tonight made me realize how wrong I was not to go back to Spain to celebrate the Barcelona Olympics.'

Staged in 1992, the Barcelona Olympics were twenty years ago, the year they had met. Danny placed a hand on Luis's leg.

'I asked you at the time. You said you didn't want to go?'

Luis admitted, 'Yes, that is what I said. And I was a fool. Those Olympics were special for Spain. It was my country announcing itself on the world stage. And I missed the party. But that's what is so great about tonight, because you seized the opportunity. I was with you tonight, living through you, and an old wound inside of me healed.'

Danny said, 'When I was walking to the station I thought – this experience doesn't become real for me until I share it with you. That's how I'll understand it, by listening to you, by watching your reaction. I had a sense that it was a special thing and now I know why.'

Inspired, Danny jumped up and approached the baby-faced guy in charge of the music, making a request for a song to be played. He asked, 'Is that a song or a city?'

Won over by Danny's persistence, he found the track and with a sceptical shrug, queued it. After a pop song finished, the sound of bells filled the room causing many to pause their conversation. They turned towards the speakers, their confusion growing as the sound was followed by a string orchestra and then, after a brief pause, the voice of Freddie Mercury, singing baritone, in duet with Spanish opera singer Montserrat Caballé, one of the finest sopranos of the twentieth century. The only person in the room to react enthusiastically was Luis, who stood up, taking Danny's hands while mouthing the words which he knew by heart, indifferent to whether he seemed middle-aged and cringey. It was the unofficial anthem of the Barcelona Olympics, recorded by Freddie Mercury in the final months before his death. At the end of the first chorus, in front of everyone, Danny and Luis kissed, and it felt to Danny like a dress rehearsal for a marriage proposal.

# Chapter Eight

## *The Engagement Ring*

It quickly dawned on Danny how little he knew about weddings. He had reached middle age without giving marriage much thought either as a prospect or as a process. The truth was that as soon as he came to terms with being gay, marriage was an idea he put to one side, not merely improbable but impossible, a foreign language he never needed to learn because he was never going to travel to that destination. He would attend other people's receptions, shed a tear at other people's vows, but he never expected anyone to shed a tear at his. The first stage of anything becoming real is dreaming about it except Danny had never dreamed about his wedding, never pictured the outfits or imagined the venue, never wondered what words he might say about love.

Unable to turn to the person he always relied

on – Luis – he chose to confide in Sophie, a friend from university. She had married at the age of twenty-five and now lived in Manchester, with a house, a garden and two young daughters. She had been a geology student at Essex University and every holiday she could be found climbing the sides of volcanoes or studying desert canyons. During term-time she and Danny had been inseparable. They met in fresher's week and lived in a house together in their second and third years. Looking back, they were in a relationship of sorts, sleeping with other people, she with guys, he with guys, but always reverting to each other, unintentionally blocking each other from forming meaningful connections with anyone else. After graduation there was a recognition from Sophie that their friendship had been too intense and, diagnosing her intimacy with Danny as a problem, she had dropped out of contact. When she reappeared, several years later, she was engaged. Danny hadn't met her fiancé and during the run-up to the marriage, Sophie hadn't asked for his advice or involved him in any meaningful way. Though he was hurt, looking back, he shouldn't have taken it personally. After all, why would anyone want his advice about marriage? Over the years their friendship recovered, never to the same intensity, but they still loved each other and they would always share the helter-skelter memories of their university years.

Hearing Danny's news Sophie cleared a Saturday and

travelled down from Manchester by train, leaving the kids in her husband's care. Arriving at Euston Station she looked ready for adventure, wearing frayed Maharishi cargo pants with embroidered samurai warriors on the back, matched with a simple white shirt. Her trainers were scuffed, her hair artfully dishevelled, she never wore perfume yet always smelt great and when she hugged Danny he was transported back in time.

'So, you're finally getting hitched?'

Danny asked, 'It is crazy, isn't it?'

Sophie shook her head.

'What's the difference? Between being married and the way you guys are living right now?'

Danny was struck by the question. 'That's what I want to find out.'

Since it was a sunny day and Londoners were always so happy when it was sunny, they decided to walk rather than catch the tube, ambling through the quaint side streets of Fitzrovia, passing small shops which sold nothing more than music scores and rare violin rosin. Sophie thought it was smart to ask for help since the jewellers might exploit Danny's ignorance as an outsider, a man trying to wangle his way into a marriage club he didn't feel part of, and she was worried that he would pay over the odds to compensate. For a start, he didn't even know whether both halves of the couple received engagement rings. Researching the subject online Danny discovered that in over ninety-five per cent of proposals only the woman received a ring. The man wore nothing to mark his engagement. Of course, it was down to Danny to figure out how these traditions translated when there were two guys.

'It feels odd that Luis will be wearing an engagement ring and I won't.'

Sophie's solution was to buy one for himself as well but Danny scrunched his face up at the idea.

'I can't buy my own engagement ring. It would be like buying my own Valentine's card. And Luis can't buy me one because I'm asking him to marry me. You wore the ring because Harry asked you. Harry didn't wear an engagement ring.'

On that point Sophie agreed.

'Yeah. But it always bothered me. And when you look at the history of engagement rings they're symbols of ownership.'

Danny cut in, 'Let me stop you there. I don't want to hear a bad word about marriage. Not today. I've been telling myself those stories my whole life to take the sting out of the fact I would never be married. Today is pro-marriage propaganda only.'

Sophie accepted these instructions.

'Got it. Positive vibes only. But that doesn't mean you have to do this like everyone else.'

Danny disagreed.

'Except I want to do it like everyone else. That's the whole point. To do this by the book even if the book wasn't written for people like me.'

On Wigmore Street they found a Swedish bakery which smelt of saffron and cinnamon. Waiting for their coffees Sophie asked Danny where they were starting their search and he suggested Bond Street. Sophie wasn't convinced this was a great idea.

'This is not a negative remark but a practical observation which is my job today. Agreed?'

Danny agreed. Sophie continued, 'Those famous brands pay to be featured in romantic movies, the ones where the hedge fund guy rents the entire store and escorts the bride-to-be inside, blindfolded, and they turn on the lights and there are rows of twenty-carat diamond rings and he says pick one, money no object.'

Danny had watched all these movies.

'And then she marries the guy with no money?'

Sophie was impressed. 'My point is that they've paid to make their brands synonymous with the dream of a perfect marriage. But they're not.'

Danny accepted this.

'I know. It's dumb. I'm a sucker. But I'm never going to step foot in those stores otherwise. I'm never going to have that movie moment. This is my chance. And I want the experience of asking to see their engagement rings, having them laid out for me, even if it's only for a few minutes.'

Sophie ventured an observation.

'This is a big deal for you, isn't it? I mean you could just rubber-stamp the relationship one afternoon in a simple ceremony in a town hall.'

Emphatic, Danny shook his head.

'We're not going to sign a few documents in the back of a rundown register office like it's a grubby secret. I want traditions. I want spectacle. I want to a make a show out of our love story.'

Referencing his failed theatrical career, he added, 'Might be the only show I ever get to stage.'

Heading towards Bond Street Sophie asked a question that had been on her mind.

'Why didn't the two of you marry when they introduced civil partnerships? When was that again?'

Accepting it was a fair question, Danny talked through the reasons.

'The law passed in 2004. Ceremonies began in 2005. And we spoke about it. At the time. But it was strange. Speaking about it. It wasn't romantic. It felt academic. We were going to have this thing called a "civil partnership" because the government told us we could. We couldn't even call it a marriage. And once you start discussing it, the politics of it, the meaning of it – there's no spark. No fire. If we were going to do something we were going to do it because we wanted to. Not because we were allowed to or because the government permitted it.'

Sophie asked, 'What's changed?'

Danny stopped walking.

'I changed. I want this.'

Sophie arrived at the most important question of all.

'Why?'

For the first time Danny formulated his desire into words. 'Because I want to stand up in front of all the people in my life and say this is the man I love. I don't want to reach the end of my life never having done that.'

Caught by the simplicity of the reply Sophie fought back her tears.

'I can't wait to be there.'

Chapter Nine

*No Breakfast at Tiffany's*

Danny and Sophie began their search at the top of Bond Street, walking down towards Piccadilly, passing some of the world's most prestigious stores, intimidating spaces with bright lighting, buffed marble floors and moneyed clientele unfazed by the sky-high price tags. In contrast, Danny's wide-eyed enthusiasm was a give-away that he was a new-comer. He had smartened himself up for the day, wearing ironed cotton trousers and a short-sleeve Paul Smith shirt which he tried to tuck in, but which came free, rebelling against his efforts at respectability. As a pair they looked like backpackers who, after many months on the road, had decided to splurge the last of their holiday cash on a fancy hotel, wearing their only vaguely smart clothes to sip vodka martinis at a rooftop bar.

The entrance to the Tiffany store was guarded by a gym-sculpted security guard dressed in a tight black suit to show off his imposing physique. Peering from the opposite side of the street Danny and Sophie loitered nervously. Sophie observed, 'Posh places prefer you to make an appointment.'

Sounding defeated before they had even begun Danny replied, 'Maybe we should go somewhere else?'

Sophie shook her head.

'No way. Tiffany was number one on your list. Come on, we used to gate-crash places with tougher bouncers than this guy.'

Danny noted, 'But we were always drunk.'

Taking Danny by the arm Sophie led him towards the entrance and after looking them up and down the security guard opened the door. Inside Danny observed several couples seated on purple ottomans in semi-private cubicles, each with a sales assistant presenting jewellery on velvet displays. It was closer to a boutique hotel lobby than a regular shop. A glamorous Tiffany representative approached.

'There are no available appointments today. We recommend returning at a time when we'll be able to assist you. Is it for wedding rings?'

She evaluated them as a straight couple, not rich but aspirational, searching for an entry-level ring, clueless on cut and carat, relying entirely on the brand – an easy mark. Sophie looked at Danny and smiled. Except he didn't see the funny side. In a hurry to correct the mistake, fearful that he was somehow undercover when he should be proudly announcing that this purchase was for a gay wedding, he said, 'I'm looking for an engagement ring. For a man.'

The assistant repeated the words.

'A man?'

Danny nodded.

'A man, yes. My partner is a man. I'm marrying a man.'

Sophie added, wryly, trying to defuse the tension, 'In case you missed it, he's marrying a man.'

The assistant struck a placatory tone.

'I'm sorry. We don't sell engagement rings for men.'

Danny took a moment before blankly stating, 'I don't understand.'

Appreciating the sensitivity, she lowered her voice.

'Tiffany doesn't sell engagement rings for men.'

After a silence Sophie was the first to regroup, her good humour evaporating.

'You sell rings, don't you? Rings that men can wear? A ring that a man could *say* was an engagement ring. I mean, once the customer leaves the store, you don't follow them around telling people it's not an engagement ring.'

Feeling that she had done her best, the assistant crossed her arms.

'You can certainly buy any ring you wish and give it to whoever you choose. I'm simply trying to explain that

Tiffany doesn't sell engagement rings specifically designed for men.'

Danny asked, 'Why not?'

The question perplexed her.

'They don't exist.'

'In this store?'

'In any of the stores on this street.'

With the heat of humiliation spreading up his neck and into his cheeks, Danny wanted to grab Sophie's arm and run out. Instead, he managed to politely say, 'I guess we won't be making an appointment then.'

With that, the assistant glanced at the security guard to indicate that this couple was leaving.

Back on the street Danny took out his vape and inhaled deeply, blowing a plume of strawberry-flavoured vapour into the air, hoping to expel some of his humiliation with it.

'Didn't Audrey Hepburn's character say — *nothing bad can ever happen to you in Tiffany's*? Guess she never tried to buy an engagement ring for a fag.'

The two of them slow-walked towards Boucheron and De Beers although there was no chance that they would continue their search with any of the prestige brands or heritage houses. In fact, Danny wanted to call the search off altogether. Sophie countered, 'I admit that was a setback. But I did some digging before I travelled down and I discovered an independent jewellery designer. I already rang her and made it clear on the phone that it was for two guys. It turns out that she's gay, but that's not why I chose her. I love her work. She started out selling in Covent Garden Market and she did so well she opened her own store. I know you wanted to do this by the book, conventional and main-stream, but how about we queer-stream this operation and end up with a ring made by someone who's excited for you rather than someone sneering at you.'

Danny remembered the real reason why he had asked for Sophie's help. She was brilliant and she never gave up. He kissed her on the cheek.

'I don't think *queer-stream* is a word.'

Sophie seemed disappointed and asked if he was sure.

'Pretty sure.'

Changing the subject, Sophie lowered her voice as if to share the most scandalous piece of gossip.

'Remember the necklace Audrey Hepburn is wearing in *Breakfast at Tiffany's*? When she's eating the pastry out of the paper bag? Well, that necklace is *Chanel*.'

Danny smiled for the first time since being expelled from the jewellery store.

'Shall I tell that to the security guard?'

With defiance they locked arms, leaving Bond Street behind them. If they wouldn't be sold a ring, they would make their own.

# Chapter Ten

## *What Will Luis Say?*

The independent jeweller's was a sliver of a shop squeezed in between a tattoo parlour and a Japanese-owned hairdresser's on D'Arblay Street. More workshop than shopfront, in the window there was an industrial steel desk from a defunct factory in East Berlin, fitted with a counterbalance lamp and a magnifying glass. A bronze bell over the door announced Danny and Sophie's arrival to the shop's security – a copper-coloured German Shepherd. A woman in her fifties emerged from the back, wearing wire-rimmed glasses and an abattoir-style leather apron, her fingernails sparkling with shimmering gemstone dust as though she had been butchering stars out back. Sophie took the lead, offering her hand which the jeweller accepted, recapping their phone conversation. The jeweller turned to Danny, introducing herself as Abi, aghast that they had wasted their time on Bond Street.

'Why did you bother? The attitude. The inflated prices.'

Danny pointed out, 'We didn't even get to the prices.'

Sensing her task was to turn the mood around, Abi pivoted.

'Listen. No one loves weddings more than me. I married my wife before civil partnerships existed. We held our own commitment ceremony in Devon in an apple orchard. I made our rings. An artist friend of mine wrote our wedding certificate in sumi ink. Okay, it wouldn't count in court, but it means the world to us. When we were finally allowed to turn it official, we applied for the legal documents, but we don't hang those on our wall. The certificate my artist friend created, that's the one we framed.'

Abi indicated for the three of them to sit on mismatched steel stools and asked what kind of ring Danny was looking for. At a loss, Danny shrugged.

'I don't know. I've no idea what an engagement ring for a guy should be. I've never seen one. In real life or in a movie.'

Abi waved away the pop culture references.

'Forget the movies. Forget the magazines. This is your wedding and your ring. We're going to create it from your mind. Did you bring a photo of Luis?'

Danny took out his phone and showed her a selection of photos of the two of them. Abi nodded.

'*Definitely* marry this guy. He's stunning. Does he wear any jewellery?'

Danny thought on the question.

'He owns a silver crucifix which his grandfather gave him. But he never wears it.'

Abi correctly deduced that Danny had no idea about Luis's ring size. Seeing him worry, she put her hand on his shoulder.

'You're not the first guy who doesn't know their partner's ring size. Is this engagement a real surprise or a pretend surprise?'

Danny thought hard on the question.

'We've been together for twenty years. It will come as a surprise.'

Abi cleaned her glasses.

'Sir, it would be an honour to make your engagement ring. But you'll need to do some detective work. You're going to have to measure his finger with string when he sleeps.'

Danny turned to Sophie.

'Is this what Harry did?'

Sophie shook her head.

'He asked one of my girlfriends.'

Abi consoled Danny.

'I know how you're feeling right now, like you're tiptoeing through these traditions as if you were an intruder in someone else's house. But you are not an imposter.'

Abi stood up.

'I'm going to brew some coffee. We're going to smoke a joint. And then we're going to talk precious metals and gemstones. Afterwards, I'm going to make you a ring worthy of a twenty-year relationship. And I swear to God, Gollum will be chasing you down the street for it. How does that sound?'

Danny opted for a seven-millimetre-wide ring. Nine millimetres felt like conforming to some unspoken notion that a man's engagement ring should be broad. As for gemstones Abi described how a diamond could be cut flat and flush-set into the band like a floor tile. When Danny saw examples of diamonds cut this way the appearance reminded him of the magic rings a sorcerer might wear and his greatest fear was that any part of this marriage should be mocked as a gaudy pastiche. Keen on the symbolism of the world's most durable precious metal, Danny chose platinum for the ring itself which was more expensive and less ostentatious than gold. He then worried that the ring seemed plain. Abi floated the idea of shaping the platinum so it would look like the gnarled roots of an ancient tree. It would be a difficult task requiring additional labour. The final cost was four months' salary, wiping out most of Danny's savings. What was he saving for anyway? He bought his clothes second-hand and the mortgage was almost paid off. The ring would be ready in time for the August Bank Holiday – the weekend he planned to propose.

Afterwards Danny treated Sophie to lunch at a tiny French restaurant on Lexington Street with antique tables, wooden banquettes and vases of snapdragons. The summer set menu was radish leaf soup, followed by morel mushrooms served on rye toast, finished with a lemon and polenta cake. Emboldened by a carafe of house white wine Danny asked, 'Why did you disappear after we graduated? You didn't tell me about Harry until you were engaged.'

Sophie turned towards the window, watching the passers-by before answering, 'Because no one I dated was ever good enough for you. Whenever I met someone, you would find fault with them. Not in a mean way, you were being protective. But the trick when you're dating is to discover if the great stuff outweighs the stuff that's not so great and to do that you need to give people a chance.'

Danny apologized.

'I'm sorry, Sophie. I had no idea. Maybe I was trying to be funny or trying to impress you. It was university. We were young, stupid and high most of the time.'

Sophie countered, 'One of the reasons people go to university is to find the person they're going to spend the rest of their life with. We didn't realize it because we were messing about so much. We wasted our chance.'

Danny asked, 'On each other?'

Sophie took his hand.

'We were never going to get married, were we?'

Danny ventured, 'Was I jealous?'

Sophie shook her head.

'You were afraid of being alone.'

Danny sat back in his chair, recalling those days at university. The conclusion hit him hard. He could critique a relationship, but he couldn't create one. Sad at the memory of that lost and lonely young man, he asked, 'Would you have told me any of this if I wasn't getting married?'

She pushed back, 'Would you have asked?'

There was silence for a time. Sophie sipped her wine, before matching his boldness with a frank observation of her own.

'When you told me you were going to propose to Luis, I admit I was surprised. After today I understand a little better what this wedding might be for you.'

Treading carefully, Sophie continued, 'It's an opportunity. To ask the questions you never asked. Of me. Of yourself. With the biggest question of all being to Luis. *Will you marry me?*'

Danny knotted his fingers together.

'I want the world to know that we're more than just two people living together who split the bills and share the chores.'

Sophie reacted sharply to that idea.

'No one thinks you're just two people living together.'

But Danny disagreed.

'That is how it feels sometimes.'

Turning to the subject of the proposal, Sophie asked, 'Can I give some advice? About the proposal? Make sure there's no one watching, no band playing, no string quartet.'

Pondering the suggestion, Danny asked, 'You think Luis might say no?'

Sophie was taken aback.

'That's not what I meant. Even if you're excited and you're going to say yes, you want the space to make the decision for yourself. You don't want to feel like you're being rushed or taken for granted. I have a friend and she was asked onto the London Eye by a guy she'd been seeing for a year. He had rented an entire pod, there was a team of people serving champagne and canapes. At the highest point he got down on one knee and asked her to marry him. Instead of thinking about him or love or whatever, she noticed that the staff were looking away, none of them were watching because they'd been instructed this is how to behave when he proposed. She realized that these strangers knew before she did. In that pod she was the last to know.'

Danny admitted, 'My greatest fear is that it will feel phoney and fake.'

The waiter filled their wine glasses and cleared their

dessert plates. Once he had left, Sophie ventured, 'Why did you ask if I thought Luis might say no?'

Danny shrugged.

'I was reacting to what you said.'

Sophie shook her head.

'You were reacting but not to me. Danny, you guys have discussed marriage, right?'

Danny's voice became brittle.

'I told you. Luis and I discussed civil partnerships as a possibility when the law was passed. Luis didn't feel the need.'

Sophie pushed the point.

'You've never spoken about it again?'

Danny thought back over the years. There were hardly any occasions when the subject had come up.

'When gay marriage passed in Spain, we discussed it. He said the same thing. He didn't feel the need.'

Sophie asked, 'Danny? Is there a chance he might say no?'

Danny considered Luis's many extraordinary qualities. He was an outsider from the south of Spain who through grit had made his way into an Oxbridge-dominated law firm, a man who saw photos of mountain ranges in *Condé Nast Traveller* and pointed to their summits and said let's go there and they did; they stood at the point where his finger had pressed against the page. The truth was that if he wanted to be married, they would be married.

'Yes, there's a chance.'

# Chapter Eleven

## *The Proposal*

Danny arranged a hiking holiday in Scotland for the last weekend of August, following the West Highland Way. He and Luis would trek from the village of Milngavie, walking around twenty miles each day, and on the fifth – after the climb out of the village of Kinlochleven, with views across Ben Nevis, the highest mountain in Scotland – Danny planned to propose.

In preparation he browsed the Piccadilly bookshops flicking through titles such as *Marrying on a Budget* and *Marriage Step by Step*. Without exception these books were written with the bride in mind. Marriages between two men or two women weren't discussed except in one recently added afterword which declared that the same advice applied whether you were straight or gay. A nice idea which didn't ring true to him. Purchasing one of the guides, he read it cover to cover in a café, over iced coffees and a slice of poppy-seed cake. In the section dedicated to engagement the author cautioned against proposing in places that were faddish or famous, recommending 'locations with permanence', their phrase, to symbolize longevity. Danny mused that since he and Luis had already achieved longevity this symbolism was superfluous.

One of Luis's favourite pastimes was trekking. Arriving at the summit of a mountain he would sit on an outcrop of rock, reluctant to descend. Luis preferred the world above the clouds; Danny preferred the world under the water. As a couple they had hiked the Cantabrian Mountains of northern Spain, the Paramillo del Quindío ascent in Colombia and the Cerro Castillo circuit in Chile, adventures that Danny would never have dared to embark upon alone. Apart from a school trip to the World War One battlefields in France he hadn't left the country until he was nineteen years old. He joked that he owed Luis the world, or he owed his world to Luis. Both were true. Since they often went on short breaks at the end of August there was nothing unusual about making these holiday plans, so Luis remained in the dark as to the real reason behind the trip; the surprise would be total.

To help with the logistics Danny employed a travel agency specializing in Scottish Highland walks. Though the trek was self-guided the agency would arrange transportation of their heavier bags between guest lodges and book their accommodation, which often sold out in the summer. Danny had explained that they were two gay men sleeping in one room – not friends, colleagues or hiking buddies. He'd have enough on his mind hiding the engagement ring; he didn't want check-in drama, twin beds, sniggers or side-eye. The agency was supportive; the manager could vouch for the guest lodge owners personally, claiming they welcomed visitors from all over the world. It was a strange comment, Danny thought, since being gay wasn't a nationality, but he let it slide, listening as she reassured him that he and his 'boyfriend' would have the hike of a lifetime. Luis was almost fifty years old. Danny was looking forward to calling him 'my fiancé'.

On Thursday 23 August, with a one-day head start on the Bank Holiday crowds, Danny and Luis caught the nine-thirty train from London Euston due to arrive in Glasgow Central Station by the early afternoon. After reading his Spanish newspapers, Luis slept for a time, resting his head against the window as the countryside rolled by. This was their first holiday of the year. A pattern had developed over their life together, the pair often arranging their breaks during the low season when prices were lower and popular locations were less busy with families, an arrangement that had always seemed advantageous. More recently it had begun to bother Danny as though it implied unmarried gay couples were expected to keep a separate calendar. Perhaps that was part of the reason he wanted to propose on a summer Bank Holiday.

When Luis woke up Danny handed him a water bottle, dented from their expeditions around the world. He took a sip while Danny explained that they were north of Preston, closing in on Carlisle and the border. Luis asked about Danny's disturbed sleep last night – he'd woken up in the middle of the night and cried out. Danny didn't want to talk about his anxieties in case they hinted at the proposal. However, the nightmare, on the surface, didn't reveal anything.

'I've had it before.'

Luis pressed for the details.

'I'm in my school swimming pool. It's a normal class except I see a door in the wall that wasn't there in real life, like a prison cell door. I climb out of the pool, walk over, turn the handle and pass through. On the other side is a mirror copy of the school swimming pool except this pool is empty, no students, no teacher, no noise. The air is cold. The water is still. I notice somebody submerged in the deep end, so I dive in to rescue them only to come face to face with myself. The dead-me is fixed in a silent scream. That's when I wake up, screaming for real.'

Luis put his hand on Danny's leg.

'Maybe you'll never have that dream again.'

The observation surprised Danny. The nightmare dated back to his schooldays and recurred at times of stress. He presumed it would be with him until the day that he died. He asked why Luis thought it might stop.

'Mine stopped. In my nightmare I was on the beach in Cádiz, on lifeguard duty, and someone out at sea was struggling so I ran into the water to save them but when I reached them, they pushed me away. They wouldn't let me touch them. And they drowned. I returned to the beach and everyone from my town was standing there asking why I had let that man drown. And I told them – he didn't want to be saved by me.'

Danny asked, 'When did it stop?'

Luis replied, 'After I met you.'

Danny had booked comfortable accommodation for their first night in Glasgow, at the Blythswood Square Hotel, an elegant row of converted Georgian townhouses. After five hours on a train Luis was keen to stretch his legs and spend the afternoon exploring the city. As a traveller, Luis's view was that adventures were infrequent and though people often believe that one day they might return to see the sights they missed they almost never do. His go-to case study, quoted like legal precedent, described how, on his twentieth birthday, he went trekking in Nepal with his best friend from school. The pair of them reached the end of the Langtang trek where they attempted a day hike without ropes or a guide, scrambling up mountain scree to peer across the snow-capped ridge towards the Tibetan border. Halfway up, his friend felt sick, possibly from the altitude and, unable to ascend any higher, Luis escorted him back down to the trekking lodge, forgoing his chance to see over the mountain into Tibet. Safely in the lodge his friend promised that one day they would return together to complete this climb. But after Luis came out, his friend cut contact with him. All Luis could think was that he had given up a glimpse of Tibet for that guy. As a result, whenever he travelled, he drew up lists of the most important places to visit to avoid feelings of regret. 'Imagine you'll never come back, and there are no second chances,' he would say. Danny was more than happy to follow Luis's lists. Over the years they had taken them to temples, ruins and summits. On this trip he hoped Luis would realize that marriage belonged on their must-do list, that it too was one of life's great adventures not to be missed.

First on Luis's Glasgow itinerary was the Gothic cathedral, the oldest building in the city. Luis and Danny avoided talking about faith – like they avoided talking about their families. Afterwards they enjoyed a lecture on Scottish whisky at a local distillery. While Luis asked smart questions Danny became tipsy drinking the free samples. That night at a restaurant recommended by the hotel for its locally sourced ingredients, including Highland deer and loch lobster, Luis spotted an omission in their itinerary.

'On the final day of trekking it looks like we're not climbing to the top of Ben Nevis? Is that right?'

Danny had been so fixated on the proposal he had forgotten the summit. Luis took out the map, unfolding it.

'It seems crazy to miss the views. Don't you think?'

Danny nodded. Luis's finger moved across the map, illustrating a possible new route.

'If we start early from Kinlochleven we can reach Fort William by midday. We then head to Achintee. From the Visitor Centre we follow the path to the top. An easy fix.'

Picking at his food Danny began amending his plans. He couldn't propose at the summit of Ben Nevis, there would be hundreds of tourists. They would cheer, clap, film it on their phones, post it online under the header 'Gay Wedding Proposal at the top of Ben Nevis!' No, he would find a secluded spot before the climb, on the route from Kinlochleven to Fort William. In his mind the proposal had been the summit, metaphorically speaking. Now it would be overshadowed by an actual summit. Having lost his appetite, he put down his fork.

*

That night Danny and Luis had sex and it was perhaps a little perfunctory but it had been a long day and Danny wouldn't have read anything into it except for the fact that he was about to propose. What did it mean to ask someone to marry you if the best years of your sex life were in the past? Perhaps he needed to accept that this was a reality of marrying so late into a relationship and he shouldn't make a big deal out of it. After the passion and athleticism of the first few months, the sex had become more vulnerable and emotionally intense as they began to trust each other more. Luis grew up believing fleeting anonymous encounters were the only possibility for gay men. In contrast, Danny always preferred waking up with his dates since they were often better company in the morning, the conversation was truer over cornflakes than it was over cocktails, revealing glimpses of their hopes and fears before they raised their defences and braved the world. His challenge had been that the more he wanted them to stay, the more they wanted to leave. Until he met Luis, he truly believed that he was a one-night stand and nothing more. A single-use body.

Looking back, the years after Luis and Danny moved in together were the high-water mark sexually. More than beautiful bodies and dirty talk, sex had been an expression that they were a team. They discussed everything and tried most things. The most vivid sexual memories were at the weekends in between redecorating the apartment in their partial shell of a bathroom or kitchen with torn-down walls and exposed wires. It felt the same way between them – torn-down barriers, simultaneously building a home and a partnership. Abiding by a conventional chronology it was the point at which they should have married. Danny wondered if marriage would create a new high-water mark or merely make them nostalgic for the one they'd missed.

While Luis slept Danny lay awake, restless in the unfamiliar hotel warmth, bothered by too many blankets, pillows and the fact that he had neglected the summit from their plans. He was about to get out of bed to open the window when Luis woke, sensing that Danny was ill at ease. Without a word, understanding what was required, he stood up, opening the window and allowing in a breeze, standing naked by the window as the temperature dropped. Once the room was cool, he returned to bed.

'Better?'

Danny agreed.

'Better.'

Luis lay an arm across Danny's chest and fell back to sleep. And out of nowhere the thought occurred to Danny that the real reason he was asking Luis to marry him was to find out why he would say no.

# Chapter Twelve

## *A Fuss*

On the third morning their Highlands hiking holiday hit a snag. August was peak season for midges, swarms of biting bugs Danny figured could be held at bay with insect repellent. But these midges were ferocious and for whatever reason they concentrated on Luis. The bites were so persistent they sought the guest lodge owner's advice, who sold them an old-fashioned bottle of Avon 'Skin So Soft' bath oil which he claimed was used by the British Special Forces training in the Highlands. Luis had lain on the bed while Danny tended to each bite, rationing the small tube of hydrocortisone cream, carefully daubing each red dot while trying not to focus his attention on Luis's ring finger now swollen with welts. Neither of them had slept with Luis in discomfort and Danny preoccupied with the question of whether he should delay or cancel the proposal.

Thankfully the oil proved to be an effective protective barrier. The sticky layer made it impossible for the midges to attack and Luis treated being greased up with good humour. Danny joked that despite being middle-aged they had discovered a new kink. With magnificent views in prospect and a clear blue sky they hoped the difficult period was behind them. The walking was magnificent, made more pleasurable by the fact they were only carrying a small backpack between them, with the day's provisions, grilled cheese sandwiches and home-baked oat bars. Danny was paranoid about losing the engagement ring which he hid in the first-aid kit as Luis was unlikely to open it since he trusted anything medical to Danny.

After twenty miles they arrived at the Bridge of Orchy, their resting point for the night. Both were in better spirits and eager to shower, rinse the oil from their bodies and enjoy a hearty dinner, looking forward to an unbroken sleep. Adding to their improved mood, that night's guest lodge was an ancient granite-walled farmhouse, the most charming and characterful so far. At reception a woman checked their details against her handwritten register. A note was affixed to their reservation. As she read it her mood elevated from professionally polite to exuberant. She explained that she was allocating them the most romantic room in the farmhouse with views of Beinn Dorain. Insisting on personally escorting them to their room, she mentioned that one of her close school friends was gay and that he had stayed in this room with his boyfriend and they had found it suitable for 'all their needs'. It was so earnest and kind-hearted that Danny stifled a laugh. As soon as they were alone Luis asked why she was behaving that way. Danny confessed, 'I spoke to the travel agency. I let them know that we're a gay couple. I wanted to make sure no one had an issue with it.'

Luis countered, 'Except you made an issue out of it.'

Ordinarily Danny would defuse most disagreements; he hated arguments and rarely felt the need to be proven right, but on this subject he dug in.

'It's better than dreading the moment of check-in when they expect us to take separate rooms or separate beds. In Cairo we changed hotel.'

The manager had refused to give them a room with a double bed, offering them a ground-floor room with twin beds facing a rubbish-strewn alley, when they had paid for a Nile-view room. He told them the hotel was overbooked and when this was queried, he suggested, if they were unhappy, they could stay somewhere else. They would not be refunded. They had left, losing all their money. Remembering the events, Luis nodded.

'Once, in twenty years of travelling, one bad experience.'

Danny said, 'Luis, she was sweet. She was nice. She was—'

Luis cut in, 'She was nervous. You put her on edge. You put me on edge. And I know that I'm tired. But I'm also tired of always being confronted with *it*. I'm tired of *it* always being an issue even when we're halfway up a mountain in the middle of nowhere.'

His use of the word 'it' made their sexuality sound separate to them. Danny tried to keep his voice steady, but he was no longer in control of his passions and the words tumbled out.

'Maybe when it goes wrong those times upset me more than they upset you.'

Moving towards the bathroom Luis declared, 'If you're always trying to stop something bad from happening, you're always going to be defined by it.'

Irritated by the condescending tone, Danny shot back, 'I am defined by *it*!'

This caused Luis to stop at the bathroom door.

'But I don't need this hiking holiday to be defined by it. I don't need the Highlands to be defined by it.'

With that said, Luis stepped into the bathroom.

Danny perched on the end of the bed, citrus oil and sweat beading on his cheeks like synthetic tears. Mist crept into the valley, pooling at the base of the mountains – impressive, if he had been in a good mood, but right now it felt foreboding. He couldn't explain that the real reason he was being hypervigilant was because he wanted the proposal to go perfectly, except his hypervigilance had provoked a conflict he wanted to avoid. And Luis was right, he couldn't incubate them from the world. It was a fool's errand to try. He was still watching the slow creep of the mist when Luis stepped out of the shower, clean and calm, kissing Danny on the side of his head.

'I'm sorry.'

But all Danny could think about was the idea that he had made a fuss. Luis might see a wedding the same way – as an unnecessary fuss, questioning the point of an expensive and time-consuming ceremony which would achieve nothing more than legally rebranding them as civil partners, a compromise label that they had rejected eight years ago. Luis didn't want to be defined by *it*. Civil partnership would define them. It was possible that Danny had placed too much value on the tradition of surprise. He should have tested the waters. Yet traditions existed for a reason. Marriages were proposed, not debated. You were supposed to be able to read your partner and make the call. Danny had made the call.

# Chapter Thirteen

## *Will You Marry Me?*

On Bank Holiday Monday, 27 August 2012, twenty years, six months and eight days after they first met, Danny was going to ask Luis to marry him. The forecast was for light showers, clearing eastwards during the afternoon, but Danny wasn't troubled by the prospect of rain. They had overcome far bigger obstacles to reach this point and anyway, there was romance to sheltering from the weather. By the time the clouds cleared and the sun broke through they'd be engaged. After all the doubts, Danny became so excited he could barely make a dent in his immense Scottish breakfast of spiced Lorne sausage served on a white bap. When Luis asked why he wasn't eating Danny answered that he couldn't wait to reach the summit. Luis tilted his head, curious as to why the response sounded like a non sequitur.

After the steep climb out of the village of Kinlochleven the path rose above the low-lying clouds, Luis's favourite place to be. Despite their relative seclusion and their early start the route to Fort William was dotted with hikers. To avoid turning the proposal into a public scene, Danny ventured off the main path under the pretext of searching for a vantage point for photographs. They climbed towards a rocky outcrop, at times on their hands and knees, reaching a granite ledge. With wisps of cloud settling on the lower slopes, the mountains appeared to be steaming as if the landscape had been recently forged and plunged into the freezing loch waters. Opening his rucksack, ostensibly for his water bottle, Danny removed the ring box while Luis stood nearby admiring the view. The showers softened to a drizzle and Danny stepped forward, joining Luis at the edge. He had imagined going down on one knee but in the moment the gesture seemed inauthentic and when Luis turned to him, expecting to be handed a water bottle, he saw, instead, the open box and the platinum engagement ring gathering spots of Highland rain.

For a time Danny couldn't speak, unsure whether he would be able to utter the most important sentence of his life. He was convinced that if he opened his mouth he would start to cry, which he had promised himself he would not do until he had heard Luis's answer. The question should be asked flat, in a steady tone, without emotion, applying no pressure on the other person. Eventually he found the composure to say, 'Luis, will you marry me?'

In this moment Luis's green eyes appeared enormous. With an inscrutable expression he lifted the ring box out of Danny's hands, no doubt playing back the past couple of months like a reel of celluloid, examining each frame for missed clues.

During the protracted silence, the thought popped into Danny's head that he should've asked the question in Spanish as well as English. He had never learned Spanish since there was never any chance of him catching up with Luis's English, but for occasions like this he could've at least learned the phrase. Maybe the reason Luis was taking so long to answer was that he had always imagined being asked in Spanish and hearing the words in English, in the middle of the Scottish Highlands, maybe it was all too foreign – marriage, the mountains, being offered an engagement ring as if he were the bride-to-be.

Desperate for Luis to speak, Danny waited as Luis looked up at the sky and then down again.

'Okay, Danny. Let's get married.'

And that was it. Luis was a world-class lawyer, eloquent and persuasive in a language that he had made his own. Were those really the best words he could manage to the world's most romantic question? Danny had expected more. But what? Some new sensation – a jolt of electricity, as if the assorted limbs of a loving union might be lifted into a higher state of being by the lightning strike of a proposal. He was being silly. The question was plain. Yes or no. It was best answered plainly. Luis had said yes.

Luis placed the engagement ring on his own finger. Technically that was Danny's job, but he had lost control of the ring box. And what was he supposed to do – snatch it back? The fit was good; the nights of secret measuring with string had paid off. The ring looked right. They kissed, their first kiss as fiancés. Danny waited for the jolt he had hoped for. But these seconds felt like the previous ones. Or perhaps, a little worse, anticipation replaced by anticlimax. The only sound Danny could hear was the wind through the trees and over the rocks as if the mountains were whispering about them.

Part Two

# Autumn

# Chapter Fourteen

## *The Engagement Party*

Their straight married friends claimed the purpose of an engagement party was to bring the two families together except Danny and Luis didn't have families to bring. After coming out they were both estranged from their families and they had long since resigned themselves to this fact. Yet Danny remained keen on the idea of an engagement party as a way of drawing together their separate social threads. Anyway, why should they give up this chance to throw a party? Luis wasn't sold. The wedding was the party; he didn't understand the point of a party to announce a party. It seemed excessive, expensive and self-congratulatory. Danny was sensitive to accusations of excess – he had faced them his whole life, too much emotion, too many hand gestures, too much sway in his walk or too many colours in his clothes.

It came as no surprise that his wedding preparations, despite being over a decade late, might be described as 'too much', as though he were planning to serve glitter-filled cocktails on the backs of swans.

Secretly Danny worried that without the ripples from a splashy announcement their engagement wouldn't feel real, existing only in their minds as a hazy Highlands memory. There was a risk that they would slip back into their regular rhythm and routine, allowing the planning to drift until the engagement became nothing more than a promise that they would one day fulfil. Sure, Luis would be wearing a ring, but a case could be made for spending two years planning the wedding – *to take their time.* Except the very last thing Danny wanted to do was to take his time. They had done that already. After moving slowly, he wanted to move fast, like a child sprinting downhill. It was September, his heart was set on a summer wedding with the engagement party as a starting pistol.

Agreeing to keep the party unfussy and informal Danny selected Village Bar on Wardour Street, the place where they had met, which felt meaningful because who would've thought, back then, that a legal union of *any* kind would one day be allowed. Though not a night for solemn speeches, Danny planned to say a few words, wanting to tell the story of how, on that bitter February night, he claimed not to be waiting for anyone when the truth was that he had been waiting for someone his whole life and that someone was Luis.

# Chapter Fifteen

## *Plastic vs. Glass*

On the evening of the engagement party Danny arrived early to check the venue and immediately began to worry that he had misjudged the event. On the walls were sultry posters of muscular men wearing jockstraps and biting their lips. On the tables were miserly bowls of mixed nuts, a lone almond in a sea of salty peanuts. But the detail that bothered Danny the most was the prospect of drinks being served in red plastic cups. This wasn't a student house party. His friends were grown-ups with careers and businesses: he couldn't ask them to toast their engagement with a plastic cup. The weary manager replied that he had supervised hundreds of these parties with older people, younger people, serious, or silly – it didn't matter who they were, glasses were always smashed and if Danny wanted glassware he would need to put down a deposit.

Determined his guests should be able to clink their glasses, Danny hurried to the cash machine near Soho Square taking out two hundred pounds, plunging his account deeper into an overdraft from the ring and hiking holiday – paranoid that this marriage might be perceived as the fake plastic version of the real thing, his mind looping the lyrics from Radiohead's classic song 'Fake Plastic Trees'. He returned to the bar with the cash clenched in his fist as though he had won it in a backstreet poker game. After carefully counting each twenty-pound note the manager said, 'Glass it is.'

At this point Luis turned up clean-shaven with a smart haircut from one of London's oldest hairdresser's, a historic establishment in Mayfair which counted Charles Dickens among its lists of patrons. Luis was an expert at collecting tokens of British identity which he wore on his sleeve like Scout merit badges. Standing in the doorway, surveying the space, he appeared serene, wearing a Dunhill burgundy top and black Burberry trousers. Danny was wearing a vintage sixties suit found in a charity shop for the sheer novelty since he never wore suits normally and wanted to show this was a special occasion. With a skinny black tie and beat-up leather shoes he looked like an impoverished artist at the opening night of his first exhibition, while Luis looked like the gallery owner. Luis walked over, taking a read of his fiancé.

'You're worrying?'

In a breathless flurry Danny listed the problems.

'They were serving the drinks in plastic cups. There are no fresh lemons. The tequila is nasty, the gin is worse. The snacks are the saddest I've ever seen. The DJ wishes he was in Miami, not some middle-aged disco. And there are naked men over the walls.'

Luis instantly ordered the problems: those which could be fixed and those which could be improved. First, he reassured Danny, 'It's going to be a great night.'

Danny shook his head.

'I wanted it to be perfect.'

Luis was struck by the word – perfect, wondering aloud what it meant. Danny's eyes darted about.

'You don't like the venue, do you?'

Luis appeared surprised.

'When did I say that? I love this bar. I've always loved this bar.'

Danny was too alert to the emotional undercurrents to let the comment pass by.

'But?'

Luis pondered whether to remain silent.

'We're not performing the greatest hits of our relationship.'

Before Danny could respond Luis wrapped his arms around him as though trying to squeeze the anxieties out of him.

'Let's go through the list. The tequila? That's an easy fix. We can pay the bar to use a nicer brand. The same with the gin. What else? The snacks. Let's replace them. We can find some better food. We have an hour. We're in the centre of Soho. We can do this.'

With an upbeat energy, Luis guided Danny out of the bar and around the corner of Winnett Street to a small Italian restaurant called Bocca di Lupo. It had opened a few years ago; he had eaten there with clients. Taking the lead, Luis launched into an eloquent explanation about how they were hosting an engagement party and the caterers had let them down. They needed platters of meats and cheeses – he knew that they didn't normally provide a takeaway service but it was an emergency and it would mean the world to them if they could help. Danny watched in admiration at how Luis won them over, something he could never have done. The owners offered a selection of cheeses including Lingotto d'Oro, Caprino and Ruoto Del Re, none of which Danny had heard of. He watched as they artfully presented a selection of thinly shaved meats including wild boar and fennel salami, decorated with sprigs of fresh herbs. Admiring the care with which they arranged the food Danny remarked, 'Who knew that cheese and meat could be so emotional?'

They looked at him as if to say: *everyone knows this*. While Luis paid for the platters, the staff congratulated them on their engagement and handed them free buckwheat crackers, the most useful engagement present they could have wished for.

Back at the bar Danny selected a smoother tequila, switching up the premade sickly-sweet margarita-mix syrup to an agave and fresh lemon mix while Luis transformed the snack table, adding supermarket sunflowers to some empty bottles of wine. With barely five minutes before the party was due to start Luis checked, 'And no speeches tonight, right?'

Danny offered a qualified agreement.

'I was going to thank everyone for coming.'

Assessing the size of the small room, Luis wondered, 'You invited everyone on the list?'

Danny swirled the drink around in his glass.

'I might have invited a few more.'

Foreseeing trouble, Luis asked, 'How many more?'

Soon there were over a hundred and thirty people packed into a space intended for sixty. Some of the guests Danny didn't even know and had never met, having encouraged invitees to bring friends, partners, husbands, wives and colleagues, promising a hedonistic celebration of love – not the low-key pitch he had made to Luis, which was a few quiet drinks with a few close friends. The free wine, gin and tequila were finished in the first hour with guests buying Danny more drinks than he could handle. Though he had vowed to stay in control and preside over the party with ambassadorial charm, by the second hour he was drunk, on the booze for sure, but also on the sheer amount of joy packed into that small room.

Among his close friends he listened to expressions of delight that he and Luis were finally tying the knot, words of admiration for their relationship that he had never heard them say aloud. Perhaps there had never been an opportunity, and he wondered if that was another reason people married, to give permission for a flood of unabashed sentimentality. Even complete strangers wanted to bask in the glow of a love story they knew nothing about either because it reminded them of their own or reignited their desire for one of their own. For a few hours that upstairs room was one of the happiest places in London.

By the third hour events became blurred, with the party turning so rowdy that passers-by heard the racket from the street. Intrigued by the scenes at the first-floor windows they entered the downstairs bar to find out if this was a special night which anyone could join and because there was no guest list and no bouncer no one was turned away.

Among the crowd Danny's theatre friends arrived, professional performers, one woman dressed in the traditional garb of a groom, in black tie and long tails with a top hat, the other a ballet dancer, a muscular man with a sprinter's legs dressed as a virgin bride in white lace with a silk organza veil. The third was a renowned Blackpool-based drag artist, dressed as a vicar, complete with dog collar and a bumblebee-blonde wig. Soon the mock bride and groom were freestyling on a tabletop with the drag vicar dancing on another table doing a Moulin Rouge can-can with her clergy frock before presiding over a mock wedding ceremony, holding a book which looked alarmingly like the Bible until it turned out to be a hardback copy of a Harry Potter title with the dust jacket removed. Danny turned to find Luis, hoping he was laughing, except he wasn't. Briefly Danny worried they were mocking marriage, that they were a group fundamentally incapable of taking the institution seriously, even at an engagement party. But before he could talk to Luis, Danny was summoned up, joining the tabletop dance, resulting in a roar of appreciation. When instructed to jump he did so without the slightest worry for his safety, carried aloft before being deposited on the floor in front of the manager who was saying something about a smashed sink.

Guided to the men's toilets Danny saw a porcelain sink had been ripped off the wall and now lay in pieces on the floor. It was so surreal, that he thought it was an elaborate practical joke, pointing out that while he had promised not to smash any glasses, he'd never promised not to smash any sinks. Luis arrived to better handle the situation, freeing Danny to return to the party where he climbed back up on the tabletop calling for silence. The room was hushed for the first time since the party began. The DJ paused the music while the guests began demanding, 'Speech! Speech! Speech!'

Danny held up his hands and cried out with the fervour of a trade unionist, 'Fuck the speeches!'

After that his memory was blank aside from one final fragment, outside in Soho at night, spinning round a lamp-post like a man auditioning for a musical, calling out to anyone in earshot, 'I'm getting married!'

# Chapter Sixteen

## *The Hangover*

The last time Danny had been hungover was after Emma and John's anniversary celebration and the contrast between the two parties was making his hangover worse. Emma's wedding anniversary was well-behaved with a lavish buffet, melon-mint cocktails, a champagne bar and articulate speeches. His engagement had been commemorated with smashed sinks, broken glasses and barely an hour's supply of finger food. Most glaringly of all he hadn't just failed to give an emotional speech, he'd mocked the very idea of them for a cheap laugh, missing the opportunity to tell his friends how much he loved Luis or how remarkable the prospect of marriage was.

Having been sick, Danny accepted a glass of sparkling water from Luis and the two of them perched on the edge of the bathtub. Danny apologized. 'I'm so sorry. I panicked. I thought no one would show up. I had this fear of telling the world that we were getting married and the world shrugging its shoulders. I don't know why I needed it to be so crowded. Or why I kept drinking. I feel ashamed.'

Luis knew the meaning of the word shame too well: waking up in the morning and converting memories most people celebrated such as sex, joy and love, into memories they tormented themselves with. Luis was stern.

'I know you feel bad right now, but you arranged a fun night for all of our friends and people were happy for us.'

Danny remarked, 'I'm just so glad Emma wasn't there.'

Luis corrected him.

'She was there. John stayed at home with the kids, but she came. She was drinking pornstar martinis with an actual porn star.'

As Danny winced, Luis added, 'She said it was one of the best parties she's ever been to. You're jealous of her parties. She's jealous of our parties.'

Danny stood up, running his face under the tap.

'Trust me, Luis: she's not jealous of us.'

At hearing this, Luis's mood changed.

'Danny, you haven't asked if I had a good time.'

Now Danny did feel shame.

'Last night all I was thinking about was whether you were having a good time.'

But Luis didn't accept this.

'That's not all you were thinking about.'

Luis walked out of the bathroom leaving Danny with the conclusion that he had failed the very person the party was intended to celebrate. After rinsing with mouthwash he followed him, belatedly understanding that Luis had been the responsible adult last night. In the kitchen Luis readied some coffee.

'The problem is you don't know what you want. You want the crazy party in Soho with strangers off the street, but then you wake up and feel ashamed because it wasn't done the right way. Except you can't say what the right way is. You want to put on a big show except who is the show for? It's not for me. It's not even for you. It's for other people. But we never cared what other people thought.'

Danny pushed back, 'Sure we did. We just pretended we didn't to make it less painful.'

Luis accepted the point.

'It was never more important than what we felt.'

Danny briefly considered questioning Luis's assertion. What other people thought had always been of paramount important to Luis. Instead, he raised his hands in a gesture of surrender.

'I screwed up. I admit it. You were right. Maybe the point of an engagement party is to screw up so we get it right at the wedding.'

Hearing this admission, Luis softened his voice.

'I have a suggestion. We hire someone. A wedding planner. You're a dreamer, Danny. I don't know where we would
be without your dreams. But turning dreams into reality is
tough. It's logistics. And spreadsheets. This is too stressful
for you on your own. You have a job with long hours; we
don't have our families helping us. We're on our own. You're
pulling in so many directions. Everything needs to be perfect but not too perfect. It needs to be traditional but not too
traditional. It needs to be respectful of the conventions but
not conventional. Fun but not funny. Hiring a professional,
someone who has done it many times, will make it more
enjoyable for both of us.'

Accepting a cup of strong black coffee Danny calibrated
his mind to the idea.

'Are they expensive?'

Luis nodded.

'But they'll save us money too. They negotiate better rates
for venues and catering. And Danny, I love you, but you are
a terrible negotiator.'

Danny knew this to be true.

'I ask the price; they tell me the price. How am I supposed
to know that isn't the price?'

Serious, Luis asked for confirmation.

'You agree that a wedding planner is a good idea?'

Part of Danny felt that he'd failed and was having responsibilities taken away from him.

'Should I be negotiating right now?'

Luis shook his head.

'No.'

Without making a conscious choice to do so, Danny echoed the exact wording Luis had used in the Highlands.

'Okay, Luis. Let's hire a wedding planner.'

He couldn't tell if Luis noticed or not.

# Chapter Seventeen

## *The Wedding Planner*

Overcoming his initial resistance to hiring a wedding planner Danny found a list of the city's top event organizers, immediately ruling out the renowned planners located in Kensington who required minimum spends of fifty thousand pounds and specialized in oligarch and celebrity weddings. Near the bottom of the list, he chanced across the website for a small company called 'Red Jacket Event Planners' which stated in their business biography that they only started planning weddings once civil partnerships became law. The offices for 'Red Jacket' were in the theatre district near Covent Garden where the supernatural thriller *The Woman in Black* was still running at the Fortune Theatre. After graduation, he had applied to work there backstage, recalling a young man with many ambitions except that one day he might be married. Located on Maiden Lane, Red Jacket shared a shabby Victorian building with casting directors. In the communal area Danny passed aspiring actors seated outside audition rooms studying monologues. He climbed the uneven stairs arriving at a narrow corridor with a brightly painted red door at the far end.

The reception was furnished with a circular mahogany table, decorated with a vase of white hydrangeas, one day past their best, a wooden magazine rack of glossy bridal magazines and a seasonal fruit platter worthy of a still life portrait. As a first impression it announced that this company was playful yet precise with a sense of genuine delight in the ceremonies they helped organize. But the quest for a perfect wedding had begun to stir memories in Danny of the body issues he suffered as a young man, never thin enough or strong enough. Before Luis, no matter how hard he tried, he wasn't the physique other guys wanted. He was too scrawny, too quirky-looking, closer to an alley cat than a pedigree. At one point he dropped to five per cent body fat and would suffer from constant colds as if his body could tell that it was a disappointment.

A fresh-faced young man greeted him, dressed in a double-breasted red jacket the same shade as the front door. He shook Danny's hand explaining that he was the junior associate of Jasper, the founder of the company who would be with him shortly. Taking a seat, Danny flicked through the magazines which included *Bridal Monthly* and *World's Best Weddings*. He wondered if this ceremony could ever truly be co-opted for two guys if the central creative force always seemed to be the bride. Observing Danny's reaction to the bridal selection the young man retrieved a separate set of magazines called *Just for Him*, crudely produced, amateur by comparison, printed on pamphlet paper. He explained that the magazine was self-published by an Australian wedding shop, the first intended solely for straight grooms. It ran for only three editions, with a print run of a few thousand before closing due to lack of interest. Danny asked if there was a magazine for gay couples. There was nothing. The young man said, 'That's why we're here.'

Wondering why he felt it necessary to lower his voice, Danny supposed that if they were pigeonholed as exclusively gay it would be the end of their business. No planner could survive without a slice of the straight marriage market.

Exactly on time, Jasper opened the double doors to his office. Concise and compact, no more than five foot seven, wearing the same style of double-breasted red jacket as his colleague, he shook Danny's hand with the aura of a concierge from a grand European hotel, brimming with knowledge and excited to share it. Assessing his client, he observed the frayed trousers, scuffed Puma trainers and striped John Smedley sweater. More significant than his clothes, Danny was attending the appointment alone. Jasper ushered Danny into his office, guiding him away from the formality of the desk towards the sofa by the bay window. He pulled up a chair as if he were a marriage therapist, with a Moleskine notebook resting on his knee and a handsome Waterford fountain pen in his hand.

'Tell me the dream.'

Unsure what to say, Danny remained silent. He didn't have a vision for this marriage; he hadn't collected a selection of magazine clippings. Even after proposing the big day remained vague in his mind. Tongue-tied, he didn't know what to say. Jasper prompted him, 'In your email you said your fiancé's name is Luis Lagana. Which is a Spanish name, yes?'

Danny nodded.

'Luis was born in Cádiz.'

Jasper wrote his first note. Danny checked to see if the ink was red. It was black.

'Were you interested in marrying in Spain? I've helped arrange international weddings in France and Italy, but Spain also has many fantastic locations.'

Danny quipped, 'Luis would be happy getting married in a London register office next weekend if it was down to him.'

After a thoughtful pause, Jasper wrote his next note.

'Is that why Luis isn't here today?'

Danny shook his head.

'No, it wasn't that he couldn't make the time. He didn't want me to feel demoted after the engagement party.'

Curious, Jasper asked what had happened at the party. Danny summarized the drunken revelry. Jasper said it sounded like a fun night, which Danny accepted.

'But it's not what we want for the wedding.'

Jasper asked directly, 'What do you want?'

Danny was honest.

'I don't know. I don't know anything about weddings. I never imagined I'd have one. I'm worried that I'm doing everything wrong.'

Jasper screwed the lid back on his fountain pen and tapped the top against his notes, realizing that he wasn't dealing with someone who needed help with specifics or logistics; Danny needed help with the concept of weddings themselves. Affixed to the page was a printout of the email Danny had sent him.

'You and Luis have been together twenty years – that's a remarkable achievement.'

The compliment caught Danny off guard.

'But we never made a big deal about it. We just got on with life, you know?'

Jasper shook his head.

'No, tell me.'

Danny expanded, 'When we met – we'd been through

tough times, changing cities, losing our families. Our faith. I was partying too much. Luis was working too much. We were different kinds of lonely. I was lonely in a nightclub. He was lonely in an office. Being together was like being in a life raft. We clung on to each other. It never crossed our mind to celebrate. The relationship was a form of survival.'

Jasper was moved by this description, understanding its deeper resonance.

'What could be more romantic than that?'

Danny agreed, except with one important qualification.

'We're settled now. We're not lost. We have friends. A home. Careers. A life together. I don't know what we're even celebrating at this point. Except I know that I want it. A celebration. Even if I don't know what it is.'

Standing up Jasper walked to the window, resting on the ledge.

'Weddings should be an expression of you and your partner. There are no other rules. There is no right or wrong. The only weddings that struggle are the ones trying to be something they're not or the ones trying to fix something that's broken. Weddings can't make a sad person happy, or an unloved person feel loved. They can be magical but they're not magic.'

Quite unexpectedly Danny observed, 'I just have this feeling that marrying Luis might be the best thing I do in my life.'

It was hard to tell if Jasper was charmed or concerned.

'There it is. That's my brief. No frills, no gimmicks. Let's not gild this lily.'

Danny was so desperate to work with Jasper that he began to worry that he wouldn't be able to afford him. Jasper handled the issue of money with tact.

'In New York City the average spend is seventy-five thousand dollars. In Alaska it's fifteen thousand dollars. Does that mean weddings are better in New York City? No, of course not. It means the venues and catering are more expensive.'

Danny thought on the numbers.

'We're closer to Alaska than New York.'

Jasper said, 'That's a parameter not a problem. I can still arrange a wonderful wedding. The issue with the other planners is that they charge a proportion of the budget, so the bigger the budget the bigger their commission. I charge a flat rate. I have no incentive to upsell.'

Feeling overwhelmed Danny looked down at the floor. He had never cared much about money, but he would love to pay for this wedding himself rather than relying on Luis. He never felt this way about the apartment or their international travel. Luis contributed more financially because he earned more. He was instinctually fair minded and handled their finances with so much grace that the disparity was never an issue. With the apartment, Danny could make up the difference by doing more of the decorations and home improvements. With the travel, Luis was more motivated to journey to far-flung locations. But the impulse to be married had come entirely from Danny. He was leading this charge and he should pay for it.

Sensing that his mood had slumped, Jasper joined him on the sofa.

'I'm to understand that you wanted a gay wedding planner?'

Danny said, 'I wouldn't presume.'

Jasper waved this comment away.

'Tell me why.'

Danny looked out of the window.

'I don't want to feel like I'm being smuggled into a foreign country by friendly forces. Do you remember at school, when they would pick teams? For football, I was always chosen last. I didn't care about that – I wasn't proud – but when the game started and I was on the pitch, running around, I felt like such a fraud, you know? Going through the motions? And I don't want this wedding to feel like that.'

Making a deliberate calculation, Jasper allowed his impeccable façade to slip.

'Part of my job will be to navigate you around the venues who would rather not host us, the people who don't want to bake our cakes or print our invites. I'm going to match you with people who love weddings as much as I do. And I've always loved weddings ever since I was a child. My mother believed they were the most joyous ceremonies on earth which explains why she married three times. In her eyes the men never matched up to the wedding. She never said they didn't deserve her – she would say they didn't deserve that day. In your case, the opposite is true. We are building a wedding worthy of your love story.'

Danny asked, 'Have you ever been married, Jasper? Sorry. That was a rude question.'

Jasper seemed sad for the first time in their meeting.

'Unfortunately, no. I admit, it is strange arranging weddings when I haven't experienced one for myself.'

Trying to be helpful, Danny said, 'For so long we weren't even allowed to dream about it.'

Jasper shook his head.

'Except I did dream about it. I've dreamed about being married even when I was young. The law never stopped me from dreaming. And I've tried to find someone. I'm still trying. It's hard at my age, without muscles or a jawline. Working in this business doesn't help. On first dates I tell people what I do for a living and they think I'm coming on too strong as if I'm already planning our wedding, which of course I am. That's the line I tell my mother anyway.'

Danny was fascinated by the idea of his mother, who must be in her seventies or eighties, wanting nothing more than her gay son to be happily married.

'And she'd attend your wedding?'

Jasper widened his eyes.

'Attend? She would be organizing it with me. When I came out, she told me, rather than don't ask don't tell, she would *ask*, and I would *tell*. I was very lucky in that regard.'

Jasper smiled, adding, 'Notice I haven't spoken about cakes or clothes or flowers or venues. These details we can figure out later. Here's the only thing that matters – how do we make this day feel like your day and not some overpriced rehash of other people's expectations.'

Danny couldn't have wished for a better guide. Only after signing the agreement and stepping out into the corridor did the thought occur to him that the role Jasper was playing should have been Luis's to play, the two of them hand in hand on this adventure, guiding and advising each other and perhaps Luis had sent him to a wedding planner not merely to help arrange the event but to outsource the excitement he couldn't provide.

# Chapter Eighteen

## *Choosing a Venue*

On Saturday, 6 October, Danny and Luis set out on a tour of prospective wedding venues with Jasper lining up four contrasting options. Despite Jasper's repeated requests Danny and Luis were unable to set out clear guidelines for the search beyond the venue not being too expensive or formal. As a result, Jasper cast the venue net wide to gauge their reactions. In his experience someone not saying what they wanted rarely meant accepting anything.

On a crisp morning with frost on fallen leaves the three of them gathered outside the crypt at St Etheldreda's, Holborn. Meeting Luis for the first time, Jasper shook his hand, taking measure of the groom-to-be and assessing the pair as a couple. Though he didn't say a word, Danny blushed, conscious that their love story was being evaluated. He couldn't help but feel that they came up short. He couldn't say why. After pleasantries were exchanged, Jasper declared, 'I've never planned a marriage where the couple have been together for so long. When the two of you met no gay person *anywhere* in the world was allowed to marry. No civil partnerships, no marriage, nothing. You're a bridge from one era to another.'

Luis wryly observed, 'How about we marry on a bridge?'

Jasper took the suggestion seriously.

'The only one worth marrying on would be Tower Bridge. It might be possible. Up on the walkways between the two towers with the sun setting over the Thames. How does that sound?'

Danny put a hand on Jasper's shoulder.

'He was joking.'

Jasper was amazed.

'Luis, why so deadpan? Give me a little clue. A wink, a nudge.'

Despite living in London for much of his life Danny had never heard of the crypt at St Etheldreda's before. It was over six hundred years old, Jasper explained, a historical site popular with school visits while supplementing its income by hosting private events such as mock medieval banquets with wenches and cheeky lute players where guests feasted on roast boar and drank tankards of mead. For medieval-themed weddings, some grooms and brides dressed up as kings and queens. Each to their own, Jasper pointed out, establishing himself as a defender of weddings in all their shapes and forms.

As they walked in Luis expressed his confusion at the urgency of needing to find a venue so soon when summer was eight months away. Jasper explained, 'We're not early. We're late. Many venues are reserved over a year in advance. Remember, everyone wants the weekend slots and there are only fifteen weekends in the summer. It's the reason that more weddings are scheduled in the autumn and winter. Too many people chasing too few places.'

Luis accepted this reasoning but remarked, 'We don't have our hearts set on any prestigious locations.'

Jasper widened his eyes.

'I'm glad you feel that way because the famous places are already booked. Today we're viewing more unusual places. But if I may be so bold – there's unusual and there's the bottom of the barrel, so let's be deliberately unusual rather than merely late and last.'

At the musty crypt doors, Jasper stopped, raising his hands like an elegant traffic officer.

'Before we begin, please remember that I have nothing at stake in your decision except your happiness. I work for you. I don't take kickbacks. I'm happy to show you any location. That said, there is a luxury hotel chain owned by a foreign royal family in a country where they execute people for being gay and those ballrooms I won't show. A puny act of protest some might say, but what kind of Red Jacket would I be without a few red lines.'

Danny asked, 'Do many couples want those venues?'

Jasper lamented, 'They're spectacular spaces in storied hotels. Many couples are looking for validation that their marriage is special. I've lost business because of it. But it's not much of a protest if it doesn't cost you anything.'

He presented them with a pamphlet.

'My associate put together these fact sheets on our venues today. Quick question. Do either of you mind marrying at the site of troubling historical events? Executions, torture, betrayals, murders – that sort of thing.'

Danny pointed out, 'It's not particularly romantic.'

Jasper sighed. 'That's so often the problem with history.'

Exploring the crypt Danny touched the sloping stone walls that were once palace foundations, his eyes following the colossal timber beams supporting the stone ceiling. Jasper asked, 'Can you imagine your wedding in the same place that Henry VIII celebrated his marriage with Catherine of Aragon?'

Luis rebutted, 'Didn't that marriage end in divorce? And schism from the Catholic church?'

Danny observed, 'Luis is Catholic. Being gay was his break from the Church.'

Surprising everyone, the comment provoked a heartfelt

response from Luis who up until this moment had been largely silent.

'I admit that it is hard for me to imagine a wedding that doesn't take place in a church. When I was growing up everyone married in the church where they lived. Afterwards we celebrated in a local restaurant. There wasn't a long list of eccentric locations to choose from. What am I supposed to think about this place?'

Recognizing the importance of the admission Danny asked, 'What do you think?'

Luis addressed him directly.

'We have no connection to this place. It means nothing to me. It means nothing to you. Are we supposed to study the history behind each venue, grasping at some kind of link?'

Hurt, Danny said, 'Luis? We can't get married in a church.'

Breaking the silence Jasper said, 'A cathedral in Cádiz is beyond even my powers I'm afraid. And yes, we're trying to find meaning and personality in one of these locations so that it feels connected to the two of you. That's the best we can do. That is our burden. We must make our own meaning. Forge our own connections. There is another way to look at this crypt – it was the location of a royal union between England and Spain.'

Luis shrugged at the well-intentioned parallels.

'It's just so random and rootless.'

Danny wondered if anywhere could match up to the image Luis held in his heart – a simple Spanish church with a traditional dinner afterwards. When he'd asked Luis to try Jasper's test, to close his eyes and picture the big day – the unobtainable scene of a Spanish church must have come to mind. He had refused to say it aloud until now. This wedding didn't feel real to Luis.

Jasper asked, 'Gentlemen, I hate to hurry you, but we're on the clock. Are we getting married in a crypt or not?'

To avoid Luis being the one to say no, Danny answered for them: 'I don't like basements.'

Luis turned to him.

'I've never heard you claim that before.'

Danny replied, 'Because we live on the top floor. And we've never moved.'

Jasper pretended to be pleased at their progress.

'There we have it. Hallelujah. Finally a preference, no basements, no crypts, no subterranean caves or nuclear bunkers. To arrive at this wedding guests must *ascend* a flight of stairs.'

As Jasper directed them out of the first venue he added, 'We're learning so much about each other. Isn't that what weddings are for?'

Jasper had intended it to sound witty but in this instance it sounded true.

# Chapter Nineteen

## *Celebration or Provocation*

Despite its name the Asylum Chapel in Peckham was never attached to an asylum but was part of the support system of almshouses for destitute workers. Built in the 1820s, burned out by an incendiary bomb in the Second World War, it stood ruined for decades before being converted into an event space and wedding venue. Danny admired the ruined stonework and the newly installed stained glass, making the case to Luis that it was a chapel for misfits and outsiders who never found a place of worship welcoming to them. But to Luis, it was an inversion of the churches of his childhood – a reminder that they were being offered architectural leftovers, while straight couples sanctified their love beneath gold leaf and centuries of tradition. Upon hearing Luis's objection Jasper clapped his hands together as though this would instantly transport them to the next venue.

At street level the entrance to the Victorian bathhouse in Bishopsgate was shaped like a submarine turret made from bricks with a spiral staircase leading down to a series of chambers lined with Arabic-motif tiles. Jasper had booked the viewing before knowing of Danny's dislike of subterranean spaces. Nonetheless he suggested that it would be useful for them to take a tour so he could assess their reaction. Once a bathhouse of repute for city businessmen, fuel costs made it prohibitively expensive and so it had been restored for private event hire. Plenty of straight couples held their wedding receptions here without giving the connotations further thought but for a gay wedding it felt like a misjudged joke. Wasn't marriage a way of banishing bathhouses to the past and dispelling a stereotype about gay men? Danny's objection bothered Luis.

'Are we getting married? Or are we running a PR campaign for the goodness of gay guys?'

Pondering seriously Danny answered, 'Aren't we doing both?'

On this theme, Jasper remarked, 'I once arranged a civil ceremony here between two men in their late fifties who were marrying for the legal protections and as an excuse to throw a party. They hated the idea that they were doing anything conventional. They embraced the history of the bathhouse rather than being embarrassed by it. They decorated the venue in the fashion of a Roman emperor's brothel. They served platters of figs and oysters and made all the guests wear togas. The couple wanted to marry but they didn't want to take marriage so seriously. And you know what? It was a great party. I discovered that nothing melts British inhibitions faster than fortified Roman wine. Of course, some of the guests looked down on them. But that was the point. It was a provocation.'

Recoiling at the word, Luis shook his head.

'It's a wedding not a provocation.'

Danny observed, 'No matter how ordinary or low-key we try to make our wedding we will always be a provocation to some people.'

From beneath the streets to high up in the skyline – the final venue was the top floor of the Swiss Re Tower, better known as the Gherkin, located in the heart of the financial centre of the City. The space was circular and surrounded by a matrix of rhomboid-shaped windowpanes offering a panoramic view. It was so sleek and science-fiction-like that it could have served as the London headquarters of a globe-trotting villain from a James Bond movie. Checking the fact sheet Jasper told them that the price was one hundred and fifty pounds per person with a minimum requirement of eighty guests. Luis said, 'We don't know eighty people. Our families aren't coming. We're only inviting close friends.'

Danny was taken aback.

'We know more than eighty people. Sophie and her husband plus their two kids. That's four people. Emma, John, their kids, five, we're at nine already.'

Luis countered, 'Most of our gay friends aren't married. None of them have kids. My point is that I don't want to look across a room and not know half the people there. We did that at our engagement party.'

Embarrassed, Danny agreed. 'We're not going to do that again.'

But Luis wouldn't let the issue go.

'The idea is to stand in a room full of people who love us. Not to fill some corporate boardroom in the sky with people who are only there for the food.'

After a painful silence, Jasper stepped in.

'The guest list is an important conversation. I'm sure you're loved by a great many people so finding the numbers is rarely a problem. Trimming the list is the challenge. Regardless, am I to conclude that this isn't the place for you?'

Danny nodded.

'It doesn't feel like us.'

Jasper agreed.

'This place is all about the view but perhaps the view at this wedding should be the two of you.'

He ushered them close, huddling like a sports team at half-time.

'Gentlemen, I could show you other locations in London. But here's my take. You both love London. You both moved here, you met here, fell in love here and you made a home here. But maybe you don't want to marry here? Listening to you talk today my professional instincts are telling me to find somewhere *outside* the city, not a manor or an estate, nothing grand but a location close to nature.'

Danny glanced out of the windows, watching the slow-moving shadows from the clouds pass over the city. One moment a street was bright, the next it was dark. When he looked back at Luis, he imagined the same darkness and light passing over his expression.

# Chapter Twenty

## *This Is the Place*

The following weekend Danny and Luis caught an early train from King's Cross Station, travelling north of London to the town of Hatfield in Hertfordshire, famous for its country manors and scenic countryside. This time Jasper couldn't accompany them since he was busy with an autumn wedding taking place in Twycross Zoo in Leicestershire. After facilitating the bride's request to feed the penguins he managed to find the time to phone Danny explaining that it was better that he and Luis experienced this next venue by themselves, advising them to cast aside the fact sheets and focus on a simple emotional question – *did it feel true to them?* After the call finished, Luis picked at the fluff on his trousers.

'Will being married change anything?'

Danny asked, 'Do you mean for us?'

Luis clarified, 'For you.'

'It must do, right?'

'Why?'

'Otherwise, why would anyone marry?'

Luis pressed, 'What are you hoping it will change?'

Trying to lighten the tone, Danny smiled. 'Luis, there's not a list.'

However, Luis remained serious.

'But you expect there to be a change?'

Danny nodded.

'Yes.'

'And you don't know what the change is?'

'No.'

'But you know that you want it?'

Understanding that more was expected of him, Danny admitted, 'When we first got together, I told everyone who'd listen that I'd met someone special. And I could see even my closest friends thinking – *let's see how long this lasts.* Because I'd never held down a relationship longer than a few months. And I would say – *no, seriously, this guy is the one.* No one believed me. In their heads our break-up was inevitable. It was just a matter of time.'

Luis pointed out, 'We proved them wrong a long time ago.'

Danny agreed.

'But the *feeling* is still inside of me. That our foundations are not as strong. Or as deep. That our love is *less.*'

Luis turned the word over.

'This wedding will make us *more*?'

'It might.'

'Give us weight?'

'Something like that.'

'In the minds of other people?'

'Yes.'

'In your mind too?'

'In my mind? No, Luis. I want what is in my mind and in my heart to exist out there, in the world – that's what I want.'

Black Rabbit Farm was a thirty-minute cab ride from Hatfield station and the taxi driver, having driven many guests to weddings there, asked who was getting married, incapable of imagining it could be the two men sitting in the back of his cab. Flatly, Danny answered: 'We are.'

Embarrassed by his mistake the driver told them how beautiful the farm was and how wonderful their wedding would be. Danny didn't speak again until they arrived at the farm while Luis made small talk with the driver to smooth over the awkwardness.

Stepping out of the taxi, Danny's bad mood was eased by the sight of his surroundings. At the end of a driveway was a limestone farmhouse. The walls were constructed from hand–cut stone held together with mortar, topped with a grey slate roof, spotted with patches of moss and wildflowers. Crooked and uneven, the fairytale building was sheltered by an alliance of ash trees. Walking forward to greet them were the owners, a couple in their early fifties, both in excellent shape with lustrous hair and lean figures. It was hard to know if they drew their health from the farm or if the farm drew its health from them. They hugged Danny and Luis with as much affection as if they were long-lost relatives. The wife was called Beth. The husband was called Noah. As they walked around the farm the couple shared their life story. They had been employed by Barings Bank, one of Britain's oldest merchant banks which, after two hundred years of profit and prosperity, collapsed into bankruptcy because of a rogue trader. Unemployed at the same time, they sold their home in Greenwich and ploughed all their money into restoring Black Rabbit Farm, making this land both their home and their livelihood, not from farming but by hosting events, from indie music festivals to weddings. They rewilded the fields and cleaned up the lake, once choked by algae and discarded scrap, now home to carp and bream. They built a walled garden using the traditional dry-stone methods where they had planted herbs and vegetables.

The threshing barn was the central space for the celebrations, far larger than the actual farmhouse, with sliding doors that could be opened if the weather was fine. Though it had been extensively renovated, the original timber beams remained. It looked like a cross between an ancient barn and an avant-garde theatre. Beth commented, 'Our chairs and tables are from a furniture maker in St Albans. Our florist uses flowers grown locally. We serve seasonal food, English sparkling wine from Cornwall, fruit from the local orchards.'

Working as a team, even in conversation, Noah added, 'We don't want to sound prescriptive or pretentious. This is your day. You pick the food, the music; you want more flowers, less flowers – whatever you want. But this farm has a soul and a character and the closer we stay to that natural character the better the event turns out.'

Surprised that both Danny and Luis were so subdued, Beth suggested, 'Let's show you the wedding forest.'

On the edge of ancient woodland was a newly planted area of trees that they referred to as the wedding forest. Noah pointed to the copper name plaques on the trunks.

'We plant a tree for each marriage we host. We moved here at the end of 1996 and opened for business two years later. To date we've planted over two hundred trees. Some couples who married over a decade ago have returned and we've hosted anniversary dinners for them.'

Walking through this forest dedicated to different love stories, Danny found the oldest tree which had been planted in the summer of 1998. He gestured at Luis.

'This could've been our tree.'

It wasn't clear if they were planning a missed wedding or an unheralded anniversary or some fusion of the two. Beth said, 'Jasper phoned before you arrived. He's one of the best wedding planners in the business. We only have one weekend available next summer and that's down to a recent cancellation. I'm afraid we have no flexibility on the date, Saturday, 20 July. If you like the place, we'd love to host your wedding. We're sure we could put on a great celebration for you guys.'

Noah agreed.

'We'll give you some time to talk alone. We'll be in the farmhouse. Stop by when you're ready.'

After Noah and Beth left Danny turned to Luis.

'What do you think?'

Luis hadn't moved from the base of the oldest marriage tree. He placed his hand against the trunk.

'I think we're getting married in July.'

# Chapter Twenty-One

## *Save the Date*

Once they confirmed the venue and paid the deposit of four thousand pounds, the largest single payment Danny and Luis had made together since the purchase of their apartment, the wedding began to take shape. When he closed his eyes, Danny could now visualize the event including where they might say their vows. He had already picked out a possible spot by the lake. After they exchanged rings, they would dine and dance in the barn.

Excited by the plans, Danny woke early one stormy Sunday morning to complete the stack of 'Save the Date' cards. He sat at the kitchen table dressed in sweatpants and an orange hoodie with only candles for light. For him, writing out the names of their guests was ceremonial rather than a chore – a ledger of all the people they loved in their life. By his side was a plate of peanut butter toast and a pot of tea. Jasper had advised him that the 'Save the Date' cards shouldn't steal the thunder from the formal invitations.

*Luis & Daniel*

*Kindly request that you*
*Save the Date*

*Saturday 20th July 2013*

*Invitations to Follow*

Taking care over his handwriting, Danny practised each of the guests' names on a sheet of paper before committing them to card, rejecting any with even the slightest imperfection. Breaking his promise to be frugal he had opted for expensive stationery, selecting a heavier textured vellum and unusual sage-green envelopes, adding a commemorative London 2012 Olympics stamp to each even though he was the only one who knew how important the ceremony had been to his decision to propose.

While studying examples of other couples' cards Danny discovered that many 'Save the Date' cards included a photograph of the couple. It had prompted a discussion between Danny and Luis as to whether they should choose a photo of the two of them. When they moved in together Danny had bought a 35mm Nikon camera to chronicle the transformation of their apartment. It was the only album he had created during their life together. But it seemed weird to use a photo from such a long time ago. Luis took photos when they went hiking using a slim Olympus Infinity camera which he slipped into his shirt pocket. He stored the prints in a shoebox, each adventure bundled together and bound by a rubber band. As they sorted through them, they noticed that they had never taken a photo where the entire point was simply to celebrate the two of them. Struck by this fact they attempted a portrait of themselves as a couple. Using the timer on Luis's iPhone they tried various poses, solemn, smiling, their arms around each other or by their sides, but the results appeared stilted. After many attempts they gave up. Danny comforted himself with the fact that at the wedding there would be a professional photographer tasked with capturing the two of them together.

Shortly after he had finished the last card, it started pouring with rain. Woken by the storm Luis entered the kitchen, noticing the stacks of green envelopes on the table.

'We could've done them together.'

Danny had worried that he would seem like a nag if he had asked for help.

'I thought it might be better if they were written by the same person. The handwriting will be the same.'

Luis didn't see the logic.

'The guests aren't going to compare the cards. No one will ever know.'

Danny couldn't deny the point.

Luis continued, 'Can I at least write one?'

Danny reached forward, selecting one of the sealed envelopes at random, opening it and ripping the completed card in half. He placed a fresh card on the table with a new envelope and a pen. Luis seemed taken aback.

'You didn't need to rip one up.'

Realizing the act had seemed hostile, Danny said, 'If you want to write one, I need to throw one away. I have plenty of spares. It's fine.'

Luis sat down and picked up the pen. Using the torn card as a template, he copied the names of the guests onto the new card. For some reason he messed up, writing at a lopsided angle. Danny handed him a new card and this time Luis fetched his own pen. As Luis made a second attempt, Danny admitted, 'There was a reason why I wanted to write all the cards. Writing them out made me realize who was missing.'

Luis looked up.

'Who?'

Danny said, 'My parents.'

Luis put down his pen. He said nothing for a time before asking, 'You want to invite them to the wedding?'

Danny nodded.

'I want to try. I'm thinking about going to visit them. To give them a card in person. You think it's a bad idea?'

Luis picked up his pen again and doodled on the ripped card.

'I've never met them. I wasn't there when it fell apart. Of course, you should visit them if that's what you want.'

Danny accidentally knocked over the stack of cards with some tumbling to the floor. Simultaneously they both knelt to collect the fallen cards, checking each to see if they were dented or marked in any way. Flustered, Danny continued, 'Isn't this wedding an opportunity? To fix the broken relationships in our lives.'

Luis sounded uncertain.

'Is that what a wedding is?'

Danny glanced at Luis.

'You don't think I should see them?'

Collecting the invitations Luis sounded stern.

'I already said you should see them. I just don't think you needed a wedding to do it.'

Danny thought on this.

'Except I did.'

# Chapter Twenty-Two

## *A Red Sticker*

Danny spoke to his parents only on their birthdays and at Christmas when they phoned each other, catching up with courteous formality as though they were former neighbours who had bumped into each other in a supermarket aisle. An unscheduled call prompted his mother to ask if something was the matter. Danny suggested that it would be better if they spoke face to face, remaining vague about his reasons for wanting to meet. His mum seemed incapable of imagining that he was returning with good news. Perhaps she supposed that he was going to tell them that he was living with HIV – a prospect his parents believed was inevitable from the day he had come out and when the joke around schools, pubs and offices was that *GAY* stood for *Got AIDS Yet*. Growing up Danny had listened to his parents instruct

the staff of their guest house to carefully disinfect any bedrooms occupied by men they suspected were gay, to double
wash the towels and bedlinens and double bleach the shower
and sink. There was a cleaning ledger and when a room
needed extra attention, either because the occupant owned
a dog or might be gay, a red sticker was added to the room
number.

Danny told Luis that it would be better for him to visit
Bude alone, to try to bridge these rifts before bringing him
to visit. His parents were professional hosts, polite around
strangers which was an awful way to describe his fiancé. But
Luis had never met them. Sitting on the bed Luis watched
him pack and asked why he didn't tell them on the phone.

'I want to see their faces. When I tell them. I want to
know if they can be happy for me. For real. Rather than
just for show.'

Luis observed, 'Is this an invitation? Or a test?'

Danny replied, 'It's like you said. When we look at our
wedding guests all we should see is affection. I don't want
anyone attending who secretly – deep inside – thinks we're
gross. For once in our lives, we get to pick the people looking at us. That's not going to be true at any other time. Not
when we're walking down the street together or enjoying a
meal. There will always be someone who rolls their eyes or
makes a comment. But it can be true for one day.'

Danny thought on the fact that they never walked down

the street holding hands. Luis knotted his fingers together, troubled.

'Danny, this wedding is not *separate* from the world. It won't take place in a better world.'

Danny refused to cede ground.

'We can make our wedding separate. We can dig a moat around it. And only lower the drawbridge for the people who truly love us. So, yes, it is a test. If just twenty people and no parents pass, that's okay. That's who'll attend. For the rest of our lives, Luis, we'll live in their world. Our wedding will be ours.'

Danny had swung from welcoming strangers off the street for their engagement party to a purity test for their wedding. After a long silence, Luis asked, 'Does that test include me?'

Stunned at the question, Danny sat on the bed, taking Luis's hands, about to deny the idea that Luis was being tested, only to find the lie wouldn't come.

'Is that how you feel?'

Luis looked at Danny, aware that his question hadn't been answered.

'I feel like I'm coming up short.'

Danny was quick to say, 'I felt that way too. But we've found the farm. We've sent the cards. It was never going to be easy.'

Luis asked, 'And your parents? What do they want from your visit?'

It was typical of Luis to reverse a line of thought and to try to see a situation from the other side, a mental discipline he had developed during his professional life. Danny was often impressed by his partner's way of thinking but now his even-handedness bothered him.

'My parents don't want anything. They didn't ask to meet me. They didn't ask to meet you.'

Luis reacted to the sharpness in Danny's tone.

'There's no point going to see them angry.'

Danny disagreed.

'That's the only point. They never understood my anger.'

# Chapter Twenty-Three

## *A Guest or a Son*

Leaving the flat the next morning, Danny experienced an anxiety he hadn't felt since they first started dating when everything was fragile and new – that he had said or done the wrong thing, that there would be no next time and that he would never see Luis again.

Danny caught the morning train to Exeter where he changed onto a regional bus. There were some seventy stops to the northern edge of Cornwall, a slow journey through the granite moors where Danny would roam as a teenager, much to the consternation of his parents who wondered why he couldn't make friends like ordinary children, concerned that he spent too much time on his own, feral in the hills or by the sea. Passing through Dartmoor National Park, six hours after departing London, Danny finally saw his childhood town of Bude.

His parents were waiting at the bus stop, both in good health from daily coastal walks and a diet of fish broths. His mum, sixty-nine years old, was wearing a brown jacket buttoned up to the neck with black trousers and sturdy leather boots. His father, seventy-three, wore a waxed waterproof jacket, grey combat trousers and modern hi-tech hiking shoes. At some point his mother had stopped dyeing her hair and it was now a magnificent grey. His father's silver hair was cropped short. For a handsome man, he had never shown any interest in style or fashion, not as the absence of vanity but as vanity of another sort, disdain for frivolous concerns. No one hugged. Perhaps they weren't sure how.

Danny's parents owned and managed a guest house overlooking the dunes. Shortly after they married which, for point of comparison, was two years after their first date, with a wedding at their village church blessed by a priest, they went into business together. They bought a rundown townhouse and converted it into a guest lodge with nine bedrooms. The rooms ranged from cosy nooks for solo travellers to a grand attic suite with sweeping sea views and a small balcony. There had been many renovations over the decades with the most recent opting for uncluttered simplicity, pine bedframes and pine cabinets, accompanied with English hospitality necessities such as mini-kettles, tea bags and home-baked Cornish fairings made with ginger, golden syrup and cinnamon. According to tradition the biscuits were given by a man to his sweetheart during courtship. Whenever Danny's mother baked a batch she would give Danny two, one for him and one for any girl he might have his eye on. Alone, he had always eaten both.

Over the years the guest house terrace had become a popular spot for visitors to enjoy homemade ice creams, celebrated for their unusual flavours such as 'Cornish Tea' with Earl Grey, chunks of scone, raisins and ripples of strawberry jam. The bar served eclectic local ales brewed with Styrian Golding hops. The restaurant made their own pasties and parsley pies. However, during the rise of cheap package holidays, the business teetered close to bankruptcy. Danny's parents had been weeks away from a forced sale with no choice but to re-mortgage their home – an end of terrace, two-bedroom house on a cul-de-sac ten minutes' walk from the guest house. Throughout his childhood the family home had remained neglected with faulty electrics, draughty windows, damp walls and a concrete backyard sprouting weeds while his parents diverted their resources into the business.

Growing up Danny would compare the condition of his bedroom to the bedrooms in the hotel, dreaming of one day sleeping in the attic suite, a room he would often clean. He would watch his parents fret over the happiness of their guests, oblivious to his sadness. He never told them how, on the daily walk to school, he was called a faggot so frequently that he had started taking a circuitous route to avoid the confrontations, entering his school over a back wall at the last possible moment before classes began. While his parents wrote handwritten notes to each of their guests wishing them a pleasant stay, Danny returned home with a note stuffed into his schoolbag from fellow students describing the various ways he should kill himself. Over dinner his parents would discuss which beach toys to buy for the summer while Danny would sit at the table, believing that it would have been better to be their guest than their son.

Arriving at the cul-de-sac Danny took a moment to admire the improvements to their home. The house was painted pale blue, the colour of diluted sky. The aluminium windows had been replaced by timber. The concrete patio was now a coastal garden with pheasant grasses, red valerian and gorse. He had followed the changes from his mother's Christmas card updates, a typed summary of the year's events, but this was the first time he had seen the transformation. He said, 'Your garden is beautiful.'

They seemed pleased.


Dinner that night was fish soup made with pollack and fresh fennel, served in their newly refurbished kitchen with its oak cabinets and German-made appliances, unrecognizable from the unmodernized kitchen of Danny's childhood. His dad opened a bottle of white wine. Danny positioned himself with a view of both of his parents.

'Mum, Dad – I'm getting married.'

His parents looked at each other. Neither of them had guessed this scenario. His dad asked, 'To the man you've been living with?'

Danny suppressed a sigh.

'To Luis, yes. Who else?'

His dad shrugged.

'You might have met someone new.'

Danny shook his head.

'Luis is the only man I've ever loved.'

The comment sounded more rebuke than romantic. They belatedly wished him congratulations. After clinking their glasses, his dad asked, 'Isn't it called something else?'

This question – the difference between a civil partnership and marriage – had been asked of Danny numerous times. Trying not to sound peevish he patiently explained, 'It's called a civil partnership. We're not allowed to call it a marriage. But we're calling it a marriage. You can choose.'

His dad said they would call it a marriage. His mum agreed.

The three of them lapsed into silence. Danny had told them about the wedding but not yet invited them. Out of nowhere, his mum began nervously telling a story.

'When I was a little girl and feeling blue my mother would suggest that we go see the bride. If there was a local wedding we would watch, even if we didn't know the couple. We would sit on the back pew, admiring the bride and discussing her dress. And it would always cheer us up.'

Danny had never heard this story before and was about to ask about it when his dad asked, 'Why didn't Luis come down with you?'

Danny replied, 'I wanted to try and fix things between us first. We're not part of each other's lives and—'

His dad interrupted, 'But, Dan, that's down to you. We're here. We're always here. You could have visited us at any time. You could have invited us to London. You cut us out of your life. You wanted nothing more to do with us. And sure, there were some difficult times. We said some stupid things. Everyone says stupid things. We were about to lose the hotel. We had a lot on our minds.'

Danny turned cold.

'I know you had a lot on your minds. Do you know how I know? Because after I told you I was gay you said – *that's all we need right now.* You lumped it together with losing the hotel. You were skint and your son's a fag. What else could go wrong? And let's be honest, that's how you felt.'

His dad admitted it.

'Yes, that's how I felt. And I'm sorry. If that's what you want, an apology, but you could've had it years ago. You didn't want it. You didn't want us. You wanted nothing more to do with us. You turned us into villains when we were nothing of the kind. If anyone is owed an apology, we are.'

Danny pushed his glass of wine away.

'Maybe I would've come down sooner if you had mentioned my relationship in one of your round-robin Christmas cards. You mention everything else. Who moved house, who bought a dog, who went on holiday. Not once did you write – Danny, our son, is living with a guy called Luis. And he's happy. That's what I was waiting for. That would've been my sign. So don't tell me I wanted nothing to do with you when you've never said a word about me.'

His mother answered, 'We weren't sure if it was our business to write about your personal life.'

Danny said, 'Maybe that's why I'm getting married so that I can finally get a mention in your Christmas card.'

A familiar kind of sadness filled Danny's heart. If this was a test, they had, as a family, failed. He left the table, retrieving the green envelope from his bag, handing it to his mum and dad.

'I came here to invite you to the wedding.'

His mother read it and passed it to his dad who put on his glasses.

'We would love to come to your wedding.'

Danny asked, unsure of his own question, 'But will you

be happy for me? For real? When Luis and I kiss? Are you going to wince? Glance at each other? Just saying you're going to come isn't enough. "Yes" isn't enough.'

The wine had made Danny tired. Noticing, his mum said, 'It's late. We thought you might prefer to sleep in the hotel. We've reserved the attic suite with the sea view.'

The three of them made the short walk over to the guest house. It was in the best condition Danny had ever seen it with handsome hand-painted signs and an extensive array of potted plants. His parents were now free of the crushing financial pressures that had shaped his childhood. They were able to enjoy their creation, so many years after they had bought it. A brisk woman from Potsdam was managing the hotel full-time. She welcomed Danny as though it were his first time here. At the bedroom door his dad said, 'I know there were tough times growing up. But there were great times too. We can choose which ones we concentrate on.'

Danny wasn't convinced.

'Maybe we can't.'

He dad looked down.

'What a shame that would be.'

Once his parents left Danny helped himself to one of the biscuits, wrapping the other in a napkin to bring back to Luis. Looking around the room, he remembered how lonely he had been as a kid here, scrubbing the sink and toilet bowl, making sure no trace of any red-stickered guest remained. He took out his phone and called Luis to make sure that he had not merely imagined the life they had created together. Danny said, 'Coming here was a mistake. Nothing has changed. I'm catching the first train back tomorrow. I can't stay. I feel the way I used to feel. And I never want to feel that way again.'

Luis said, 'Talk me through what happened.'

After listening to Luis's measured interpretation that it seemed like his parents were trying their best, Danny showered, enjoying the sea-salt scrub his parents had spent many hours testing and selecting for their guests. Sitting on his bed he found the card his parents had written welcoming him to the guest house, as if they too had always known that he would rather have been a guest than their son.

Chapter Twenty-Four

*The Terrible Thing I Never Told You*

Danny woke up unsure where he was. Instinctively he reached for Luis and, not finding him, sat up. Over the years they rarely slept apart and always with their arms around each other as they had done on their first night together. As Danny slept on the right side of the bed the hotel linen on the left was smooth and untouched. It occurred to Danny that the desire to marry might be as simple as a fear of waking up alone. He pulled back the covers which smelt of talcum powder, selected by his parents to be as inoffensive as possible. Running a guest lodge was about navigating a neutral path, creating a centre ground where everyone felt welcome. It was something he could never do – create a house where everyone would feel comfortable staying, a polarizing figure by default, excluding him from the family business before it had even been offered to him. On his way to the bathroom he opened the doors to the balcony and looked out over the sand dunes. Despite the unsettled November sky, he decided to swim in the sea.

It was a short walk to the beach, the sand streaked with lines of seaweed and driftwood after a storm. As there was no one else around Danny stripped naked, walking out into the freezing shallows before diving under the water, swimming along the seabed holding his breath for as long as possible. When he surfaced, he swam as fast as he could, suddenly tempted not to return. The pull was so powerful it took a conscious effort to stop. He trod water for a time, staring at the wide-open sea. The childhood fantasy of a kinder society under the waves no longer held the same grip over his imagination and he swam back to shore.

The hotel breakfast was porridge made with creamy milk from a local dairy and sweetened with heather honey from the moors. Afterwards Danny and his parents set out for a clifftop walk. Following their conversation last night his parents seemed to have compartmentalized the years they spent apart as something they could never fully comprehend, rationalizing it as the collateral damage of their son being gay. The family had experienced a rupture and a separation, one many parents of gay children grappled with to varying degrees. Over time a balance was found between the child's chosen family and their biological family and it had simply taken Danny longer to find that balance. But for Danny it wasn't enough for his parents to merely attend the wedding, their attendance needed to mean something more – that they understood each other better, that they had not only restarted their relationship but also remade it.

At the top of the cliffs the three of them arrived at the Storm Tower, an octagonal structure decorated with the points of a compass, designed as a refuge for the coastguard, itself now in need of rescue from a crumbling cliff edge. Seeking shelter inside they looked out across the sea at the approaching rain. Danny had set his mind on telling them about a formative event that had happened when he was young. It explained, he believed, why he had needed to escape and why it had been so hard to come back. His dad crossed his arms. His mum took a seat. Danny began, 'By the time I finished school, I didn't know anyone who was gay aside from my drama teacher. There was no internet, no chat rooms, no mobile phones. I was eighteen years old and I had never been kissed. So, I paid for a lonely-hearts ad in the local papers.'

His dad shook his head in disbelief.

'Dad, what other options were there? My friends had house parties to figure sex out. I had nothing. I collected the replies from a payphone in the visitors' carpark so it wouldn't appear on your bill. Mostly there were creepy messages but one was promising, a polite older man staying in a house close to Boscastle.'

His mum asked, 'How much older?'

Danny noticed how quick his mother was to leap on the matter of age, as if she'd always believed that being gay was a form of corruption inflicted on Danny by an older man.

'I was eighteen, claiming to be twenty-one. He was forty, claiming to be twenty-nine.'

Danny had been forced to lie since the age of consent for gay men wasn't lowered to eighteen until 1994, prohibiting Danny from having sex through his university years.

'We arranged a date on a Saturday afternoon. I studied the map, worked out how to get there. An hour and a half by bike. I picked out my best clothes, styled my hair, stole some aftershave. When I arrived, I left my bike outside and rang the bell. The man was good-looking. Neat and tidy. I had this idea that he was a teacher. He stood there, for a time, as if figuring me out. Which was odd because what was there to figure out? I was exactly who I claimed to be – an inexperienced young gay man. Looking back, he was probably calculating the odds.'

His dad sought clarification.

'The odds of what?'

'Whether I'd go to the police.'

Neither of his parents spoke.

Danny continued, 'I should've walked away. I knew something wasn't right about him. He was off. But I thought – maybe this is how men like me are when we grow up. We're all a bit off. I told myself that I was being a coward, that I wasn't afraid of him, I was afraid of sex. Which was true. The reason that I thought he was a teacher was because that's what I was looking for – a teacher, someone who could teach me what it meant to be gay. I hoped he'd sit me down, tell me the story of his life. Which was laughable. He didn't want to talk. Inside I began to shiver even though it was the middle of summer, so I said no offence, change of mind, I'm going to leave, let's do this some other time. He said I was being silly, why was I being so silly? I should have a drink. He took me by the wrist and walked me to the kitchen where he poured me a glass of red wine. I took one sip and my legs became weak, not because the drink was drugged but because I knew that I'd missed my chance to leave.'

At this point Danny's dad stood up, walking to the doorway of the storm shelter as the rains arrived, sweeping over the cliffs.

'If you'd told me, I would've killed him.'

Danny registered the violence in his reply.

'The thing is, Dad, I wasn't scared of what you'd do to him. I was scared of what you'd do to me.'

Danny had often imagined telling his parents this story, but he had never imagined the pain it would cause them. Shocked at the implication, his dad said, 'We never laid a hand on you.'

Upset, his father stepped into the rains, pulling up his

waterproof hood and setting off towards Bude. Danny leaned against the stone walls, unsure if his mum was about to leave and only the heavy rains were holding them together. But rather than leaving Danny alone in the storm shelter his mother joined his side.

'We're never going to get back the time we lost. No matter how many sad stories we tell each other.'

The pair of them listened to the rain for a time before she asked, 'What happened with that man?'

Danny shook his head. He had lost a sense of what he was trying to achieve.

'It doesn't matter. I came here to invite you to a wedding. I don't know why I'm talking about him.'

His mother suggested, 'Because they're connected.'

She was right. They were connected, as though the first encounter had been a curse, and the wedding was the spell to lift it. Danny returned to the end of story.

'After he kicked me out, I walked my bike back home. I couldn't cycle because of the pain. I remember watching the sunset and hating it. I hated everything I saw. Our house. The sea. The cliffs. This town. At home, I took a shower. Cleaned myself up, threw my underwear away, hid them at the bottom of the bin. I swallowed twenty aspirin and went to bed.'

Danny stretched his hand out into the rain, feeling the drops on his skin.

'Twenty was enough to feel like I was doing something dangerous. But not enough to be dangerous. In the morning, I didn't eat breakfast. I didn't eat for days because I was scared that I was torn inside. And I wasn't, not like that, but in another way I was. I wanted to say something. I was desperate to say something. I needed you to tell me that my future was not going to be men like that or sex like that.'

His mother contemplated this.

'I could never have told you that. You were always going to have to find it out for yourself.'

Danny nodded.

'That's why I'm here. That's what I wanted to tell you. That I found my answers. That I'm no longer torn inside. And I don't want to be angry anymore.'

Arriving back at his parents' house Danny found his dad waiting for him at the kitchen table with a photo album open. He gestured for Danny to take a seat.

'We made a lot of mistakes. But it was never about shame. We were afraid for you.'

Danny couldn't count the number of his gay friends who had heard similar sentiments from their parents. It was never disgust, they would claim. It was concern for their children's health or their careers, a fear that they would spend their lives alone. Much of the world will hate you, they would warn, some people openly, most privately, if they bothered to think about you at all. And how could any parent be happy about their child being hated when they only wanted the best for them. But the conversation took a different turn when Danny's father said, 'We should have told you the truth about your grandfather. I was scared that what happened to him might happen to you.'

Danny had no idea what his father was referring to.

'What are you talking about? He died in a traffic accident before I was born.'

His father's voice became quiet.

'No one believes your grandfather's death was an accident. No one who knew him well. He died on a dangerous stretch of road, but he'd been cycling his whole life. He knew these roads better than anyone. And the driver maintained that my father swerved *into* the impact.'

His dad allowed that fact to sit before adding, 'The insurance company investigated. There was no suicide note. Everyone in town claimed he was happy. He was popular. He was loved. They paid out, which is how your mother and I managed to start our business. But there were always doubts.'

Sensing the direction the story was heading in, Danny asked, 'What kind of doubts?'

His dad nodded.

'After his funeral I cleaned out his study. My father loved to travel, which was not common back then. He kept travel guides from different cities. I found them, hidden behind his other books. They were called *Bob Damron's Address Book*. Have you heard of them?'

Danny shook his head.

'They were the first guidebooks published for gay men. And my father owned a few including for San Francisco, Los Angeles and New York.'

Danny asked, 'He was gay?'

His dad shook his head, but then changed his mind and shrugged.

'I don't know what words to use. He was married to my mother. I'm his son. He was a pillar of the community. Daniel – I burned those books. All of them. I told your mother and no one else. They were evidence of a fraud.'

Danny wondered if his father was referring to the fraud of his grandfather's death or the fraud of his life.

'Why didn't he burn them?'

It was a good point and one his dad had wrestled with.

'I wish he had. Only recently I began to wonder if he wanted me to find them as a way of explaining why he left without saying goodbye. He was living two lives. He be-lieved there was more value in his death than in a life like that.'

Looking directly at Danny he said, 'You remind me of him. His gestures. His physicality. The way you would go for long runs, he would cycle for many miles. And I was scared when I saw him in you. I thought history might repeat itself and that you would grow up with that same sadness inside of you. I tried to set you on a different course. And I see now that was the exact course my father was on.'

His father offered Danny the photo album. Danny studied his grandfather's face for traces of himself.

In town they bought flowers from the supermarket. The only half-decent bunch remaining on a Sunday afternoon was a bouquet of mauve carnations. The three of them walked to St Michael's cemetery, not far from the centre in the grounds of a nineteenth-century church. Passing the tombstones of the fishermen and sailors who perished off the coastline's rocks they arrived at the grave of his grandfather. Danny laid the flowers and said, 'Hey, Granddad.'

As if they were meeting for the first time.

# Chapter Twenty-Five

## *A Suggestion*

Arriving back in London late on Sunday evening Danny found Luis reading in his chair. All the lights were off except for an antique floor lamp – discovered in an auction, formerly from a department store. The unusual bronze stand branched around the bulb in the vague approximation of a heart. If it had been deliberate, it would've been tacky, but the impression was an accident of the design and Danny didn't even mention his observation to Luis for fear the sentimentality might spook him. During the long British winters Luis read under it most evenings, making it one of Danny's most successful gifts and seeing Luis under it gave him a misjudged burst of confidence.

'I have a suggestion,' Danny said, before hello. Luis placed his book on his knees, taking off his reading glasses, observing Danny's energies were elevated, as though he had bounded up the stairs, eager to share urgent news. They had been messaging throughout the weekend so Luis was aware that the visit had gone better than expected and that Danny's parents not only wanted to attend the wedding but also wished to meet beforehand, proof of a wedding's healing power. There was an idea that Danny had held back from discussing on the phone, wanting to say it face to face and he blurted it out before he lost courage.

'On the train back to London I was thinking maybe you should do the same. Return to Spain. Speak to your mother and your father. Invite them to our wedding. I'm happy to travel with you. I just thought, why not? I learned so much. This is a chance to—'

Luis closed his book with a snap, cutting Danny off. He stood up, moving out of the light and into the darkness.

Belatedly, Danny realized that he should have taken a few moments to better assess his partner's frame of mind – to ask how he was, how his weekend in London had been. Luis's parents had always been off-limits. A third rail in their relationship. Trying to backtrack, Danny said, 'Luis, it was just an idea. If you don't want to go to Cádiz, that's your decision. I respect that. If you don't want to speak to your mother or your father, I understand. I was scared too.'

When Luis replied his voice was clipped and cool. Danny was unable to see Luis's face.

'Do you know who you sound like when you talk about marriage? A convert who's found religion late in life. Not only is marriage the answer to all your problems, it's also the answer to all my problems – it's the answer to every problem. Tell me. What happens if we follow every convention? What do you win?'

Danny said, trying to make peace, 'I win you.'

But Luis rejected this as glib.

'You already have me. You have all of me.'

The pent-up frustrations from the past few months broke loose as Danny answered.

'Do I? Because it seems like you're on the sidelines, watching me arrange everything, as if this wedding were only for me.'

Without missing a beat, Luis said, 'This wedding is only for you.'

The two men were silent for a time. Their most serious arguments were often the quietest. Luis hadn't intended to talk to Danny in this way, but perhaps this was the only way, provoked unexpectedly, the honesty of a reflex response. Trying to pull his thoughts into a calmer and more coherent argument, Luis said, 'Danny, we live together, travel together, eat together and sleep together. The truth is that we've done everything together except for this marriage. Which you're doing on your own, for reasons of your own.'

Misinterpreting this as an olive branch Danny moved closer.

'So be more involved. Luis, that's what I want. More than anything, I want you to be a bigger part of it.'

Luis shook his head.

'I can't be.'

'Why not?'

'Because it's not a wedding. It's a midlife crisis.'

Danny realized he was holding his breath.

Luis explained, 'These past few months have felt manic. You haven't been sleeping. You wake at four in the morning to write save-the-date cards. And if even a single letter is crooked, you rip the card up. You spent all your savings on an engagement ring. At the engagement party you were jumping off tables and shouting at strangers in the street. And I've been waiting for it to settle down, but it's only become more intense.'

Danny closed his eyes. He had experienced events like this before – a rip in his reality. Such as the night he realized that he was homeless. Marriage had been a kind of madness. He had done a great deal of talking these past few months. It was time to listen. Luis's voice began to waver.

'It doesn't feel like a celebration of our life together. It feels like a test. Am I as excited as you? Am I laughing as much? Changing as much? I would prefer if you just said – I'm not enough for you anymore.'

Luis put down his book and turned to the window.

'When you proposed, in the Highlands, the first thought that came into my head was not that you wanted to marry me. But that you were breaking up with me. And because that idea is so painful you couldn't say it with those words so you said it with the question – will you marry me?'

Danny broke his habit of rushing to speak and took a moment to plan his reply.

'Luis, I can't imagine my life without you. This marriage is because I love you.'

Luis stepped close, placing a hand on Danny's arm, the first moment of contact during their exchange.

'I know that you love me. There isn't a day where I doubt it. That's not what we're discussing. We're discussing whether this is the beginning of something. Or the end of it. Is this a marriage? Or a midlife crisis?'

Unsteady on his feet, Danny took a seat in Luis's reading chair, as if it might better help him understand.

'I admit that I've been a lot to deal with these past few months. Too intense. I don't know why marriage has become so important to me. I want our relationship to be recognized. I want it to exist in law. I want anniversaries, a photograph on the mantel, honeymoon stories. All the sentimental stuff that I mocked and ridiculed, I want it.'

Luis nodded.

'Because you feel something is missing. But it's not a

honeymoon or an engagement ring or even a wedding. In your head you've searched for what it might be, and you've decided it's marriage, but what if marriage is a stand-in for something else?'

Danny asked, 'Like what?'

Luis replied, 'Whether you want us to be the only love story in your life.'

Danny understood he was being asked to peer deep inside their relationship and tell Luis the truth. He stood up.

'Luis, part of you is still in the closet. You've outsourced being gay to me. You're still the insider. Without me by your side, who would know? And that's how you like it. It's not that you're not *out* enough. You're not *us* enough. When I asked you to marry me, I was asking you to wear our relationship all the time, not just when we're together – not just when you clock off. Even when we're apart.'

As he was trained to do, Luis reduced the marriage to a motive.

'You were sad in the summer. And out of that sadness came this proposal. You asked a question, but the question was not will I marry you. The question was – will the next twenty years be like the last twenty years. And you've already decided that they can't be the same. You've been presenting this marriage as a way to repair the past. Except the truth is – it might be your way of escaping the future.'

Plotting a potential path out, Danny said, 'Couldn't this

be a marriage and a midlife crisis? We both have a break-
down. We pick up the pieces. We build something new.'

But Luis said nothing.

Danny asked, 'Are you leaving me?'

Luis raised his hands.

'That's the question I've been asking for months. Are *you*
leaving *me*?'

Part Three

# Winter

# Chapter Twenty-Six

## *Leaving*

With only two leather holdalls, Luis had packed enough clothes for ten days. Danny hoped this meant he was coming back soon but Luis couldn't say for sure. Standing in the hall Luis was ready to leave, except wasn't marriage supposed to be their next adventure or had separation been their destination all along? For the past week they had spoken frankly but never with the same friction. For Danny, the marriage fever had broken, while Luis seemed lighter, finally able to express himself freely. Well-versed in the rhythms of a closeted life, for Luis their engagement had followed a similar pattern, pretending everything was fine while feeling removed, as if watching the process from behind a pane of glass. Close but never connected. Talking late into the night, Danny accepted that he still clung on to a sense of worthlessness, that it was possible he found self-loathing comforting, he was so accustomed to it, and that deep down he was still a young unloved man sleeping rough on a park bench. No matter the course of their conversations Luis always returned to the idea of going home. Ironically, Spain was Danny's suggestion – the trigger for the confrontation. Luis accepted there were matters from his past that he had never addressed. Marriage was the moment to face up to the trauma he had migrated from. Danny had been brave. It was Luis's turn.

At random moments during trivial tasks Luis seemed close to tears, remarkable for a man who rarely cried. Danny had always sensed the outlines of pain sheltering inside Luis. He remembered him crying at a French movie when, on screen, a kid was given a blue bicycle. Luis couldn't explain why and afterwards they had laughed about it. Who was this semblance of a successful man broken down and who would he be put back together? From the outset Danny hoped to sail their relationship to an undiscovered country but now that they were at sea, he longed for the familiar shoreline they had left behind. He had been reckless to upend such a good thing, unappreciative of his good fortune in finding any kind of love, gambling it all for what, exactly?

Before leaving for Spain Luis arranged to stay with Emma and John in their Cotswolds cottage for the weekend. Luis wanted to spend some time with John talking honestly about whether coming out placed a ceiling on his career. He had been working obsessively, giving up weekends and evenings, holidaying only once a year, as if trying to compensate for that admission so early in his career. He could have easily brought a woman to their wedding. Would he now be part-ner if he had? In his weaker moments, Danny couldn't help but interpret Emma and John's generosity as a conspiracy to separate them because they never truly believed that he was good enough for Luis. In his darker hours he imagined them whispering critiques of his character and short-listing eligible men. But Danny accepted that these were predicta-ble insecurities – the very anxieties that had driven him to plan a splashy wedding.

At the front door Danny panicked that Luis was about to hand over his keys or take off his engagement ring. When he did neither Danny declared, 'I proposed at the point most couples file for divorce.'

Luis shook his head.

'This isn't a divorce.'

Danny agreed.

'You have to be married before you can be divorced.'

Luis asked if Danny would be okay.

'I'll be okay,' he said, sounding brave. When Danny asked him the same, Luis bit his lip.

'I don't know.'

Luis always seemed to have an answer and strangely it was soothing when he admitted to having none. Danny offered

Luis space and time – he wouldn't chase him for updates or ask how he was doing. He wouldn't message multiple times a day. Luis could call home at any time. He could come home at any time, but he would not be interrupted with questions or queries. Danny compared their process to a patient going under general anaesthetic, placing the relationship in a sedated sleep and when the remedial work was complete the relationship would awake, and their life together would continue – stronger. Fixed. Except there was a chance these two broken men were together precisely because they were broken.

Standing at the door, Luis and Danny were unsure how to leave each other. Since moving in together they had never been apart longer than a few days. Breaking the impasse Danny hugged Luis goodbye, trying to keep his grip loose so that it didn't seem like clinging. With his voice muffled by the fabric of Luis's coarse coat, he said, 'Promise me that when you're ready you'll come back. Whatever you decide.'

Luis nodded.

'I promise.'

But Danny wasn't so sure. He remembered swimming in Bude and the irrational impulse to continue out to sea. Luis picked up his bags and walked out of the door, descending the stairs without a glance or a wave. It wasn't that kind of goodbye.

# Chapter Twenty-Seven

## *Alone*

Danny stood in the hallway, half-convinced that Luis would reach the street, change his mind and bound back up the stairs, breathlessly dropping his bags as he flung open the door, the pair of them kissing with the intensity of reunited lovers at a railway station. After a while he walked to the balcony, allowing cold air to sweep through the apartment with Luis's Spanish newspapers rustling mournfully on the coffee table. They missed him too, it seemed. At a loss, Danny tended to the plants, removing the dead leaves, collecting them in his palm before tossing them into the air and watching them fall to the gardens below in a sad imitation of wedding confetti.

Without Luis, the apartment was a place to sleep and shower, but not to linger, like a lightbulb without electricity, glass and filament but no glow. Danny boiled the kettle but didn't brew a tea. He carefully washed the dishes by hand. This was living alone, he thought. He had never lived alone. He had never learned how. For the first time in his life there was no one, no parents, no flatmates, no friends, no strangers and no Luis. Being alone was freedom, he had heard people claim. But to him it was a limitation. What did people do on a Saturday when they lived alone? Meet people, he supposed, in crowded places. But that would involve conversation and he had no desire to explain his situation. To be comforted or consoled. He would keep their pending nuptials preserved in amber until Luis returned.

Devising a coping strategy for the upcoming days, Danny planned to ask for overtime at the hospital, leaving only the thinnest slivers of time to wallow or ruminate. Satisfied with this solution, he set about requesting extra shifts. Even so, he still had to muddle through today, opting for a long run after which he would be exhausted and able to sleep. Run. Sleep. Work. That would be his life. He vowed to be in shape for Luis's return with a healthy diet, alcohol-free. He would grow stronger, not wither or weaken.

Wearing a beanie hat and thermal gloves, Danny set off across Waterloo Bridge and through the centre of town. He followed the tree-lined avenue bisecting Regent's Park, up Primrose Hill and towards Hampstead Heath, running to the rhythm of reassurances that it-will-be-okay, that Luis would surely weigh everything they had created together and return. It was impossible to imagine that on the cusp of marriage it could fall apart.

Passing the historic Kenwood House at the top of Hampstead Heath, Danny slowed at the café, busy with Saturday visitors. He remembered how he and Luis stopped here once after a stroll, one of those complacent couples oblivious to the loneliness of others. He should head back home, he told himself. Except the thought of returning to an empty apartment filled him with such dread that he continued onwards, out of the Heath, following a haphazard route, past Highgate, through unknown streets and suburbs, with no idea where he was going, towards the outskirts of the city as if he were fleeing the capital.

By dusk Danny arrived at Shenley Park, a place he had never heard of. There was a walled garden and an apple orchard. He tried to run through it but after eighteen miles exhaustion caught up and his legs crumpled. He collapsed onto his back, lying on grass stiff with the cold. The clouds were a curious colour, filthy silver lined with faint blue curves. Danny was struck by the impression of being underwater, holding his breath on the seabed, looking up at the underbelly of a glacier. He longed for the light to stay the same, for the sun to stop setting, unable to stomach the prospect of the night alone. A dog bounded over, a Labrador licking his face. The owner followed, smoking a clumsily rolled joint, the end smouldering in the gloom. The three of them watched the last light drain out of the sky.

Perhaps it was the four-hour run or the crowded Tube ride with passengers coughing and sneezing but arriving back home to an empty apartment Danny felt unwell. Barely strong enough to stand in the shower, he slumped against the tiles until the hot water ran out. After drying himself he put on a tracksuit and a thick terry robe. Even with these layers he couldn't stop shivering. He dug out a picnic blanket, cocooning himself on the living-room sofa where he lay staring through the window at the pots on his balcony. The only colour among his plants came from the heather, a single brushstroke of mauve, a recent addition inspired by the Scottish Highlands. Luis was everywhere.

Alone, Danny experienced a variation of silence new to him – his thoughts possessing a physicality, a humming in his head as palpable as the beating of his heart. He turned on the radio, hankering after the patter of conversation, not banter but voices as companions.

That night, in a dream, Danny was by Luis's side, discovering an unfamiliar location – the ruins of an ancient desert civilization. The rubble walls were black basalt, the same colour as the shadows they cast. The barren dusty landscape was Martian red. Luis and Danny carried frayed canvas backpacks full of parchment scrolls as they entered a crumbling fortification, the only man-made structure for hundreds of miles. While Luis was excited to explore, Danny worried about making it home. It was a dream so simple in its reflection of reality it was barely a dream at all.

# Chapter Twenty-Eight

## *Doubts*

Two weeks after Luis left, Danny calculated that he must have run out of clean clothes and was either washing them or buying new ones. Either way, he hadn't come home, and Danny's imaginary schedule was wrong. That night he couldn't sleep. At several points he was on the brink of calling Luis. Such a call would have broken their agreement and implied dependency. He had promised to give Luis as much time as he needed and not to demand a running commentary. Returning to Spain was more complicated than Danny's weekend visit to Bude. Luis had been estranged from his family, his homeland and even his language. Two weeks was not enough time. Danny doubled his estimate to a month. What was a month apart in the context of twenty years together? He passed the night by playing solitaire at the kitchen table until he eventually fell asleep on the cards, waking with the eight of clubs stuck to his forehead. Peeling it off, he wondered what it foretold.

At a reasonable hour Danny phoned Jasper, a substitute for calling Luis. Up until this point he had confided in no one, keeping the separation a secret, holding out the hope that Luis would return before Christmas and no one need know about their break. He worried that even the most kind-hearted friends would whisper to each other that the relationship was evidently flawed. They might conclude the marriage was a last-ditch attempt to hold together a fraying bond, a ribbon tied around a fractured bone. Jasper existed in a different category from his friends and family. He was a wedding professional and a witness to every type of trial and tribulation before the big day.

Early on a Saturday morning with a heavy mist over the Thames they met by Lambeth Bridge on the south side of the river at a small coffee kiosk perched on a wooden pontoon. They bought takeaway coffees and strolled down the pedestrian walkway towards the South Bank. Jasper was wearing cinnamon-coloured cords, a black wool jumper and an alpaca scarf. Positively funereal. Trying to put an optimistic gloss on the predicament Danny presented the separation as a natural part of their unique wedding journey. Yet Jasper was confused by the mixed messages, a plea for help muddled with assurances that everything was okay. He asked whether Danny wanted assistance with the practical-ities, such as delaying preparations. Danny shook his head. He wanted to know what Jasper made of the situation. Jasper remained cautious, pointing out that he never commented on the relationships he was professionally involved with and anyway, that it was impossible to truly understand another couple's love. Desperate for someone to talk to, Danny persisted.

'I don't want to put you in an awkward position. But I haven't told anyone else. I don't know who else to talk to.'

Hearing this, Jasper relented.

'What are you reconsidering?'

Danny walked on, kicking at the cracks in the paving stones.

'I made the decision to get engaged on my own. The next decision needs to be made together.'

Troubled, Jasper binned his coffee cup, placing a gentle hand on Danny's back as they walked.

'I owe you an apology. I wanted so much for your wed-ding to be perfect, for personal and professional reasons, that I created the impression that there are perfect weddings for perfect relationships. From where I'm standing, it's obvious that you're both in love. I don't know who you're comparing yourselves with but there isn't some higher level to achieve.'

After a time, Danny said, 'What if there is? A higher level of love?'

Jasper added, 'Can I share something? My business is struggling. The recession hit the wedding industry hard. Many marriages were delayed, scaled back, budgets were halved. My role was the first to be cut. Everything in my office appears immaculate but it's an illusion because no one hires a wedding planner struggling to make ends meet.'

Remembering the ageing white hydrangea, Danny cut in, 'Jasper, we will pay you in full, regardless of whether our wedding goes ahead.'

Jasper looked embarrassed.

'I appreciate that. And honestly, I need the money to survive. But the recession isn't the only reason my company is in a bad way. Lots of people don't want to hire me. When people hear about a "gay male wedding planner" often they imagine a comic figure, fluttering around the margins of a ceremony he can organize but never be part of. When prospective clients see that I take my work seriously, they go to the wedding planners in Mayfair. If they want serious – they hire straight.'

Danny stopped walking, leaning against the embankment wall and taking out his vape. Jasper joined Danny, watching as the mist slowly broke apart, revealing glimpses of the Houses of Parliament and the slate-like surface of the Thames.

'Danny, I've been trying too hard with your wedding because if I could create the perfect wedding for another gay couple maybe that would make me feel better that I've never created one for myself. I worry you and Luis are imagining that what you have isn't enough. Because we have always been told what we have isn't enough. But you've loved someone for twenty years. Some marriages fall apart after two. Look at me. I've never dated anyone longer than six months. And that guy was doing magic shows on a cruise ship for most of that time.'

Danny smiled for the first time in weeks.

'Jasper, whatever happens with this wedding, I'm happy to have you in my life.'

Jasper joked, 'How about this – if Luis doesn't marry you, I will.'

Danny replied, 'You'd only be marrying me for the wedding.'

Jasper pointed out, 'No, I'd marry you in an instant if it wasn't for one problem. You're head over heels in love with Luis.'

Danny nodded.

'And he's about to break my heart.'

Saying the words aloud, Danny realized that he had never been through heartbreak, never suffered a serious break-up. Never moved his things out of a home. Never said goodbye to a man that he still loved. He was forty-five years old and, in matters of the heart, still inexperienced.

# Chapter Twenty-Nine

## *A Postcard*

A postcard from Cordoba described how Luis was travelling across Spain, to some of the lesser-known towns he'd never visited. Danny read the card a thousand times. The style was plain and factual. *Love, Luis.* That day Danny tried to occupy his mind with professional problems, patients suffering far more serious concerns than his own domestic troubles. Minimizing the upheaval in his life worked well until he wondered if he had always depended on helping patients to make himself feel better. Walking home, he took out his phone and called Sophie, the friend who had known about the engagement before anyone else. As soon as she answered he said, 'The wedding's off.'

*

On the Saturday before Christmas Danny caught the morning train from Euston Station to Manchester and sat in the corner of a quiet carriage slumped against the window like a sack of post that had lost its postman. He was struck by how curious heartache was – a distress that wasn't anger or agitation, there were no tears, but a numbness in his chest. Colours dimmed. Music softened. Laughter was for other people. When the train arrived at the station, he was the last to stand, the last to collect his belongings and the last to disembark.

On the station concourse stood an artificial Christmas tree as white as correction fluid, the symmetrical branches unevenly draped with emerald tinsel and crowned with a flashing red star as if warning of an accident. Sophie was waiting nearby, an inversion of their previous train station reunion – from summer to winter, engagement to postponement. She was wearing an aviator jacket with shearling lining in the style of a pioneering female pilot from the 1930s. After three weeks of wearing scrubs at work and sweatpants at home, Danny had made an effort to smarten himself up with a black turtleneck and brown brogues. Gaunt and pale, with the air of a Parisian poet, he walked slowly. Sophie watched him approach, assessing his state of mind, correctly concluding that he needed a hug. Her fingers discreetly explored his back, checking how much weight he had lost. He rested his head on her shoulder and said nothing. When they disentangled, she locked her arm through his, as had always been her way in good times and bad, the two friends walking out of the station to the sounds of The Pogues' classic 'Fairytale of New York' playing from a nearby sandwich shop which, despite the 'faggot' slur, had always been Danny's favourite Christmas song.

They caught a bus to Eccles Sixth Form College where Sophie's two daughters, Penelope and Maggie, aged ten and eight, were training with Manchester United's Regional Talent Club. Standing on the touchline with his arms crossed was Sophie's husband, Harry, watching the practice game with as much intensity as any professional manager. A handsome man in his forties in shape from competing in an amateur football league, he shook Danny's hand and told them the score. There were other parents on the touchline, sharing Thermoses of tea along with commentary about the game, relationships as foreign to Danny as he was to them.

After the final whistle the five of them squeezed into the family's red Vauxhall Astra. The two girls peered at Danny as he sat in the front passenger seat while Sophie sat in the back between them. The girls could tell Danny was heartbroken without understanding what heartbreak was. On the drive home Harry explained that the family had tickets to see the Christmas lights at Dunham Massey, a National Trust mansion. Since it was sold out, he couldn't buy another ticket at this late stage but he had seen the lights many times and so offered Danny his ticket while he would stay at home to make dinner. Embarrassed by the generosity, Danny declined. Trying to follow the implications of her parents' hospitality and their consoling tone, their eldest daughter Penelope ventured, 'Are you sick?'

Danny turned around.

'No. In fact, I'm a nurse so it's my job to make sure other people don't get sick.'

Confident in her powers of perception, Penelope didn't budge from her observation.

'Then why are you so sad?'

Danny felt guilty at being so downcast at a time of joy for this family.

'You're right. I am a little sad. I'm sorry.'

Penelope said, 'It's okay. You can be sad. I get sad too.'

They arrived at a semi-detached red-brick Victorian house on Fog Lane in the suburb of Didsbury. While the girls changed into their favourite festive sweaters Sophie spoke to Danny.

'Please take the ticket. I wasn't a good friend after university. Let me be a friend now.'

Danny replied, 'I don't want to be that guy again. Coming to you in times of need, seeking a shoulder to cry on. This wedding was about creating a celebration. I wanted to stand on stage with Luis and for people to look at us and go *wow*, after twenty years they're still madly in love. I'm the first of my gay friends to marry. I made such a fuss about it. And I fucked it up.'

Danny wondered if Sophie would be inventive and suggest Luis's reaction might be an obscure Spanish tradition, unearthing some ancient Andalusian machismo ritual whereby it was customary for the man to spend months roaming the wilderness to prove himself worthy before returning to the village ready to be a husband.

'Danny, this relationship hasn't ended yet, has it?'

He scratched his greying stubble and didn't reply.

In the end Danny accepted the ticket to see the Christmas lights. During the drive to Dunham Massey it snowed and Sophie's younger daughter started to cry. When Sophie asked what was wrong, Maggie said she was crying because it was perfect. The mansion looked like a Christmas card. Across the historic estate lay an untouched dusting of snow. They walked the trail, the four of them holding hands, through landscaped grounds decorated with lanterns and lights. A silvery stag stood proud, briefly posing for photographs before disappearing into the forests. To warm up they sheltered in the tearoom with Danny treating them to extravagant hot chocolate piled with whipped cream and tiny pink marshmallows. Penelope asked, with a spot of cream on the tip of her nose, 'Are you marrying a man?'

Danny nodded, trying to be funny by also dipping his nose into the cream.

'That was the plan.'

Neither of the girls laughed, more fascinated by the idea of two men getting married.

'I've never been to a wedding with two men before.'

Wiping the cream from his nose, Danny said, 'Neither have I.'

As the girls puzzled over this conundrum, that he was doing something he had never seen other people do, Danny felt an instinctive unease that he had somehow spoken inappropriately, that even this conversation, not of his making, was pushing an agenda onto other people's children. He abruptly changed the subject and asked how the hot chocolate ranked among their favourites. It came in at fourth, behind a ski chalet in Switzerland, a café in Edinburgh and a bakery in Vienna. *Tough crowd*, Danny thought.

When they arrived back Harry welcomed them with the family's Christmas tree elegantly decorated with ribbons and pinecones, and topped with a chipped porcelain angel that had crowned Sophie's mother's tree and her grandmother's before that. Three generations of families watched over by a damaged angel. The house smelt of cooking. The table had been laid in their dining room. There were candles and embroidered napkins. The room was so appealing that Sophie kissed Harry on the cheek. He had cooked an oxtail stew served with oven-roasted sweet potatoes. As they ate, the girls relayed the entire trip for their father so that he didn't feel that he'd missed out. Danny hardly spoke, enjoying the respite from his own thoughts. For dessert there were deep-filled mince pies bought from the school Christmas fair, served with brandy butter. After dinner they played three rounds of Jenga before the girls were ushered to bed.

While Sophie read to her daughters Danny and Harry washed up, opening a second bottle of Spanish red wine Danny had brought as a gift, the only wine he knew anything about. A little tipsy Harry found the courage to ask about the wedding and the separation.

'Here's an opinion. And I could be off the mark. What if you guys are overthinking this whole marriage thing? Because it's new. You're taking it too seriously. Look at me. I didn't think about marriage deeply. What's to think about? I love Sophie. She's brilliant. Beautiful. She turned up when I asked her on a date. When I suggested we live together, she said yes. After a year I asked her to marry me. Marriage is just something you do when you find the right person.'

Danny listened to this description of marriage. He envied it.

'We missed our time. We're doing it out of time. I don't know why it's so different. I wish it wasn't. But it is.'

Sophie came into the kitchen and helped herself to a glass

of wine. Detecting that the conversation was at a sensitive juncture she joked, 'Whatever Harry said, I apologize.'

Remaining proud of his advice, he repeated it.

'I said it was possible Danny and Luis were overthinking marriage. That marriage doesn't need so much deliberation. It's just something you do when you find the right person.'

Sophie paused.

'You didn't think much about our marriage?'

Realizing his mistake, Harry shook his head.

'Did you?'

Sophie sipped her wine.

'I thought about it a lot.'

Turning to Danny, she added, 'Have you ever wondered if the problem is that deep down you might be conventional?'

Danny nodded.

'The thought crossed my mind.'

Harry asked, 'Why would conventional be bad?'

Danny answered, 'Because it was never on offer.'

Later that night Sophie and Danny huddled together at the back of the garden, seated on the girls' climbing frame, smoking a joint as a nod to old times. After passing it, Sophie wrapped her arms around him.

'Danny, don't fall apart.'

# Chapter Thirty

## *Falling Apart*

Arriving back in London Danny pictured Luis waiting for him at home, seated in his reading chair with a Christmas tree by his side. But there was no reason to hope for a festive reconciliation. Luis had been away for too long to believe that returning out of the blue would be a straightforward heart-warming gesture even if he did return with a tree. Climbing the stairs Danny braced himself for the apartment to be empty and it was. In contrast to the familial commotion of Sophie's house the air was frigid and still. He stood for a while in the hall, wondering if the home he and Luis had laboured over for so many years could ever be their home again.

Danny unpacked his bag, finding the card that Sophie's girls had drawn for him, a depiction of the silver stag from

Dunham Massey. He put it on the kitchen table beside a pile of unopened Christmas cards, unable to face their warm wishes for next year's wedding. It was late and he ought to go to bed, but his mind was racing and he was afraid of insomnia. Negative thoughts lurked in those sleepless hours and he didn't want Luis returning to find him broken and bitter. Saying you couldn't live without someone was romantic: not being able to live without them was unattractive.

Before resorting to the trickery of sleeping pills Danny decided to go for a run. As usual he set off over the river, skirted the perimeter of a locked Regent's Park before arriving at Hampstead Heath. With a determination to exhaust himself, he sprinted up the hill, reaching its highest point, Jack Straw's Castle, where he stopped, catching his breath. Formerly a historic coaching inn, hoardings indicated that it was soon to be developed into luxury apartments. Images of families and hybrid cars left out the fact this was the most famous gay cruising spot in the city – a place of delight and disgrace, a few of the scandals well known, many covered up. Not having walked these dirt trails for over twenty years Danny wasn't sure why he was walking them now, not from pent-up sexual desire – he had never felt less attractive. It was possible that he was pre-emptively blowing up the marriage before Luis could, to preserve some illusion of control. Or perhaps, like a man at the end of his tenancy, he was window-shopping his future.

Passing the detritus of casual sex, wet wipes and teeth-torn sachets of lube, he saw the twin shadows of two men cast by the light of a hard bright moon. Nearby a campfire was burning, reminiscent of a music festival. This underworld had grown bolder during his time away, less fearful of physical assaults or arrests from the police, a fiefdom left to its own devices. Logs had been arranged around the embers and a band of misfit men were perched on the stumps.

Approaching the fire Danny saw that one of the three men was Chris, his retired civil servant mentor from the Men's Ponds. They had never met here before. When he saw Danny he was surprised, beckoning for him to sit beside him, which he did, glancing at the other guys. One wore wire-framed spectacles, the spherical lenses reflecting the flames, a gold wedding band clearly visible. The second man was colossal in stature with a shaved head, a ginger beard, a silver septum ring and saucer-wide eyes, which explained why he wasn't cold even in torn black jeans and a tissue-thin t-shirt, a man more mythic than real, with steroid-pumped arms and a triangular back, like a lumberjack from a fairytale. No one introduced themselves yet these men already knew each other, in a way, watching the embers splutter into the night sky.

Breaking the silence Chris whispered, 'I fare better in these woods than online. Once they see my age guys on the apps want my money or my humiliation. A few want both. Sad but true: the Heath is safer than my own home.'

Guessing correctly Danny asked, 'Did something happen?'

Chris nodded.

'I was the worst kind of fool, flattered by beauty and youth. I should've known. He was too handsome, too eager. Once we were in the bedroom, he tied me up, pressed a knife against my neck, gagged me, punched me and ransacked my house. I was bound on the bed, listening to him smash vases in search of ten-pound notes. Here's the crazy part. I wasn't afraid of dying. I was afraid of being found like that, tied up like a carcass. In the end, I was saved by my cleaner. She set me free and quit. Who can blame her?'

Nervous at the question, Danny asked, 'Did you call the police?'

Chris looked embarrassed.

'No. Old habits, you know? I should have. That's what shames me the most because he will have done it to someone else. He had a taste for it, I could tell. After that encounter I deleted the apps, changed the locks and have never invited another man back to my house.'

Chris shook his head at the memory.

'Here, I feel safe. What could happen? If you call for help ten guys will come out of the bushes, outraged at this violation of our sacred space. We look after each other.

During the summer I'm the chatty old fag by the water. In the winter I'm the chatty old fag by the fire. Tending to the fire gives me a certain cachet in a caveman sort of way. And I have a weakness for cavemen.'

Danny smiled. 'Is that so?'

Chris expanded.

'Oh yes. Neanderthals didn't go extinct because they didn't know how to fuck. They were probably the best lovers this earth has ever known. Killing they were less good at which is why we ended up with a planet full of brilliant killers and lousy fuckers. What a shame that is.'

Chris pivoted the conversation.

'Do you know how many men come here not for sex but because they're alone? They sit on these logs with dull eyes and sunken shoulders. I force a conversation. I talk about a book, the weather, whatever comes into my head until their eyes perk up.'

Danny had always seen Chris this way – a guiding star.

'I'm sure you've saved a lot of people in your time.'

Chris accepted the compliment and Danny wondered if this assistance was penance for refusing to allow his lover to live with him, a balm for a lifetime of guilt.

'I'm not proud of much in my life but I am proud of that.'

Danny asked, 'How many people have you saved tonight?'

Putting his hand on Danny's knee, Chris said, 'Just one, Danny. Go home.'

# Chapter Thirty-One

## *An Unexpected Arrival*

By skipping the festive parties and working overtime, Danny rebuilt the small financial reserve spent on the engagement ring. Spent or squandered, he asked himself. His mind now existed in twin-track realities. In one universe he was marrying; in the other he was breaking up. Apart from gifts for close colleagues the only present he had bought this year in the event of Luis's return was an antique brass pocket compass from Camden Passage market, once belonging to a United States soldier from the First World War, with the letters 'US' engraved on the top – like the reading lamp, too sentimental had he asked for it. At home he would occasionally open the compass and watch the dial find north, a gift symbolizing togetherness or the search for it.

Walking to the hospital on Christmas Eve his phone rang.

He expected it to be Luis every time. But it was his mother. After sharing the news of Luis's departure with Sophie, he'd decided to tell his parents. They said little on the call, bewildered by the turn of events. Today his mother regained her customary authority.

'We're driving up to London. We've booked a room at a guest house. The owner stayed with us a few years ago and we always promised to visit.'

He heard his dad in the background gently suggesting she get to the point.

'The point is we want to cook a family Christmas dinner and since you can't come to us, we're coming to you. If you give us a tour of the flat tonight and leave us a set of keys, tomorrow we will cook a turkey with all the trimmings and it will be waiting when you return home from work. We know that you're a grown man and you'll be fine but we're on our way, the room is booked, and the turkey is in the back of the car. So, please, just say yes.'

His parents were booked into Willow Guest Lodge in Belsize Park, a red-brick Edwardian property with a hand-painted wooden sign at the gate and a Christmas tree in the front window decorated with dried citrus garlands. Welcomed at reception Danny was shown through to the musty communal parlour where he found his parents sharing mulled wine with the owner, a portly man with ruddy cheeks who wore no wedding ring. Accepting a teacup of mulled wine poured from a teapot wrapped up in a woolly cosy, Danny enjoyed the blend of cloves, cardamom, red wine and brandy. Cup in hand, he sat mostly in silence, as was his way these days, content to listen to the three of them swap stories about their strangest guests, stories which sounded affectionate rather than critical. It occurred to him that his parents must have a broad affection for people in all their guises and eccentricities, a fact that he never appreciated growing up.

After finishing their mulled wine, they set off to the nearby tube station. His mum was emboldened by them being a family again and as they walked through the sleepy backstreets she suggested they have the difficult conversation now rather than over Christmas dinner. His dad made it clear they weren't judging. They were trying to better understand.

'Is Luis your only serious relationship?'

Danny thought back on his dating history, encounters measured in weekends or weeks, except for one man who lasted two months.

'There was one man before him. At every chance he would belittle me and because he was witty, he did it in a way which made you laugh until you realized the joke was always on you. It made me fight to get a nice word out of him and when he did say something nice, I was so relieved. In the end I said, I can't do this, I might be young, I might not know what love is, but I know that it should make you feel good. I remember him saying — "who else will have you?"'

His parents were as affronted by this remark as if it had been said about them.

'You didn't believe him?'

Danny corrected them.

'I did believe him. That's why he said it. And even though I left him, I thought – he's probably right.'

His mother was upset.

'How could you believe no one would love you?'

Danny stopped walking.

'Because no one ever had. I'm not talking about parental love, or friends. I'm talking about romantic love. I'd never experienced it. Until I met Luis. I couldn't believe a man like Luis said yes to me. Maybe I still can't believe it, maybe that's why I asked if he would marry me – to see if it's true.'

On Christmas Day Danny set aside time for the patients without visitors, keeping them company while they ate their festive lunch including two slices of turkey breast so perfectly white and round it looked as though they had been carved from a full moon. Against the backdrop of a constrained budget the hospital still managed to bring some joy to the meal, adding a Christmas cracker to the tray. Danny placed paper hats on patients' surgery-scarred heads and read out the jokes. Some of the patients didn't say much. A few wouldn't stop talking. One elderly man, recuperating since late November and usually one of the most cheerful people on the ward, seemed downcast. When Danny asked if he was okay the man explained that he had been given his discharge date. He had made friends on the ward. He knew the names of every nurse, porter and patient. He took Danny's hand and begged him to intervene. He didn't want to go back to an empty flat.

Some of the nurses were wearing tinsel crowns despite a stern memo being circulated by the Infectious Diseases Department warning that Christmas decorations needed to be sterilized to avoid the risk of spreading viruses and tinsel posed a biohazard. The memo was pinned up on the staffroom noticeboard framed with disinfected tinsel above communal bowls heaped with sweets, gifts from patients and their relatives, including Devon fudge, Welsh toffee and baklava. During their lunch break Danny and his colleagues warmed a batch of mince pies in the microwave, which crumbled in their hands as they ate them. When the conversation turned to plans and the following year, Danny made an excuse and hurried out.

By the time Danny finished his shift it was dark outside, the streets were silent and almost everyone was at home, celebrating. In the gloom he appreciated his parents' foresight. They had pictured this exact moment – the sadness of returning to an empty flat on Christmas Day. Opening the front door, he heard carols being played. In the dining room the table was laid, candles were lit. His parents had driven over in the morning and brought a small plastic tree with them which they had assembled and decorated with the box of baubles from the wardrobe. There it stood, a rough copy of Luis and Danny's tree. His mother caught his gaze and realized the mistake. Oblivious, his dad declared, 'You and Luis made a beautiful home together.'

Danny told them the food smelt delicious and the table spread looked great. He asked if he could take a quick shower and change his clothes. Take your time, they said.

After a shower Danny selected his most festive outfit, a fluffy red sweater. Inspecting himself in the mirror he missed Luis so much that he was forced to sit on the edge of the bed and close his eyes. As if those emotions were being broadcast his phone rang. He reached for it, seeing Luis's name. It was his first phone call since leaving. Taking a beat, steadying his voice, Danny answered, wishing Luis a Happy Christmas. They both asked how they were doing and reassured each other that neither of them was alone on Christmas Day. Luis was with school friends in Madrid. Eventually the call thinned to silence. Danny told himself to keep things cheery and light, but his impulsive nature won out.

'Have you seen your parents?'

Luis paused before replying. 'Turns out, my parents are divorced.'

Luis sounded upset. Danny wanted to be by his side, to console him, to hear what had happened.

'I'm sorry.'

Luis remarked, 'Growing up I was desperate for my mother to leave him. Every time they argued, I dreamed of it. I hated their marriage and couldn't understand any part of it. I'm not sad they're divorced, I'm sad they didn't divorce when I was young enough to enjoy it.'

Realizing he didn't know enough to comment further, Danny asked, 'When are you coming back?'

Luis was silent for so long Danny worried the call had dropped. He could hear background noises. The sound of glasses, chatter and chairs being moved. A bar, he imagined, or a home full of people. He couldn't decide which was worse.

Luis answered, 'When I know what to say to you.'

# Chapter Thirty-Two

## *Another Year Is Over*

The mental health nurse Danny had befriended during rehearsals for the Olympic opening ceremony invited both him and Luis to a New Year's Eve party at his apartment. As if anticipating that their response would be to politely decline, Matt described the hook of this house party as access to the building's roof where they could sit on the chimney stacks and watch the midnight fireworks. Having been invited to the wedding, he had sent a big bouquet of flowers and a handwritten card in which he explained that it would be his first gay wedding, saying it would be an honour to attend. Danny admitted, 'Luis and I are taking some time apart right now.'

There was a particularly sharp pain in sharing the news with a gay friend, as if Danny had let the side down after creating such a commotion around his marriage, accepting congratulations like he'd struck a blow against bigotry. Danny didn't mind the humiliation – he'd crawled through a few gutters in his time – it was the disappointment he couldn't bear. As a group his friends were so accustomed to hearing about break-ups, addictions and the toughest of times that he didn't want to offer another sad story until it was the only one left to tell. Matt told him how sorry he was.

'But you can't stay at home alone on New Year's Eve.'

Waking up on the morning of New Year's Eve Danny contemplated the prospect of the year ahead, previously filled with appointments at prospective tailors and meetings with the caterers. After a breakfast of cornflakes which he ate so slowly they turned to mush by the final spoonful, he was eager to leave the apartment. His plan was to spend the entire day in town before heading to Matt's New Year's Eve party. Wondering what to wear he rummaged through his clothes, opting for indigo jeans, pleased that he could still fit into a thirty-inch waist. With dread, he speculated whether he would soon need to create online dating profiles – something he'd never done, filling them with statistics and specifics. He and Luis had never passed through the digital gatekeepers and Danny doubted there was an algorithm that would have matched them. He paired jeans with one of Luis's tops, an azure cashmere sweater. He couldn't decide if he was wearing it because he wanted Luis with him in some way or if it was an expression of sublimated anger. The soft fabric carried a trace of Luis's earthy perfume, sandalwood oils hand-mixed in the spice markets of Marrakech, nothing like the cheap-and-cheerful scent that Danny preferred, reminiscent of a salty coastal breeze.

At a café near Charing Cross station Danny bought a toasted poppy-seed bagel which he ate plain on the cold stone steps of Trafalgar Square, looking down towards Parliament. Keeping him company pigeons picked at the crumbs he left behind. On a whim he went into the Japanese hairdresser's in Soho, an establishment that had caught his eye when he had been buying Luis's engagement ring. His stylist was a young woman called Akemi. She studied his mass of overgrown wavy hair, auburn and grey, unkempt and uncut since Luis left. Danny sheepishly observed, 'It's a mess.'

She didn't disagree, asking what he wanted his hair to look like. Smart or Sexy. Naughty or Neat. Danny replied, 'Not broken.'

Akemi barely missed a beat, pointing at his hair.

'This is broken. You want not broken.'

During Danny's haircut they spoke about the snowfall in Hokkaido, the northern region of Japan where Akemi's parents lived. She expressed amazement that he had never been skiing. Never married, never been skiing, what other deficiencies were there? Danny had never owned a car and never kissed a woman. Gazing at his reflection he thought he looked like lousy material for a party. Cheering him up, Akemi's haircut was excellent, an artful mix of messy and styled. Somehow he did look less broken. He promised to go skiing in Hokkaido.

Strolling down Regent Street Danny studied the Christmas lights he had missed this year. With the shops closing early he decided to treat himself to a pistachio-nut ice-cream sundae served at an Italian gelateria near Green Park. The two scoops were presented in a crystal bowl with a slender silver spoon and covered in sprinkles. Realizing he was the only person eating alone Danny took out his phone and read an article about the most expensive ice-cream sundae of all time, created in New York City, draped in gold leaf, flavoured with the rarest Madagascan vanilla pods. During the past month Danny had discovered that random facts and radio shows made good companions. After settling the bill he made his way past Buckingham Palace, wishing a Happy New Year to the Queen, managing to cross Lambeth Bridge before the centre of town was barricaded by the police. Arriving at Matt's apartment early Danny offered to help set up. Matt hugged him and told him his haircut was hot. Danny asked if he was trying to look too young. Sceptical, Matt looked him up and down.

'In cashmere?'

The pair carried back eighty-eight cans of Swedish pear

cider from a nearby off-licence. With all the alcohol in the fridge Matt took Danny aside and opened his palm revealing a baggie containing small pink pills shaped like strawberries, explaining that they were Ecstasy pills, very mild, loving, and that he didn't want Danny moody in the corner. Danny hadn't touched drugs in years. Matt wondered at this.

'But Luis is Spanish. The parties over there are wild.'

Danny pointed out that Luis was from the south of Spain.

'He grew up religious, attending hour-long services on Sunday mornings, running errands, fetching fresh bread from the bakery at five in the morning. He's never done a drug in his life.'

Matt wasn't sure that these facts followed each other.

'We all started off as choirboys. What happened when he came to London?'

Danny thought about the shape of Luis's life.

'Work was Luis's obsession. He never went down any dark holes. Maybe he's doing that now? The breakdowns we all went through in our twenties. Could be, right?'

Matt closed his palm.

'I hope not. Anyway, I don't want you doing anything you're not comfortable with.'

Matt was about to put away the pills when Danny reached out and took the bag. He had grown tired with his mind. Peering inside he pinched a pink strawberry pill between his fingers and without another word put it on the tip of his tongue. He opened a can of cider and washed it down. Matt widened his eyes and checked his watch.

Aside from a gradual cider drunkenness, Danny felt nothing for the first ninety minutes. Perhaps his body was too old for drugs, the walls of his cells had stiffened and toughened like those cheap cuts of meat that chefs turned into stew. The drugs simply bounced off his rusted receptors. This proved not to be true. As the first guests arrived, they must have wondered who this odd middle-aged man was – high at ten p.m. He couldn't be sure if it was the drugs or his state of mind, but Danny found it challenging to strike up conversations with these young men. Every topic seemed so arbitrary. Danny had developed a nurse's knack for small talk but in the hospital conversation served a purpose, helping patients relax, and Danny rarely spoke about himself. At this party the words were passed back and forth like Monopoly money until Matt reminded him that if you were searching for someone to kiss, every conversation could be thrilling.

As midnight approached Matt suggested that they make their way to the roof to secure the best vantage point. They sneaked out of the party and climbed up the fire escape onto the slate roof, clambering to the central chimney stack where they took prime panoramic position facing in the direction of the Thames. They wrapped their arms around each other like a pair of Victorian chimney sweeps who were only able to express their love high above the city. With the

Ecstasy causing Danny to grind his teeth, he asked what dating was like these days. Matt said, 'Mostly it's good.'

This seemed improbable to Danny, but Matt doubled down.

'What's not to enjoy? You meet a guy from a part of the country you've never been to or a part of the world you know nothing about. The other person is a mystery. You're imagining what it means to be them. They're imagining what it means to be you. The downside is that often the people you like the most are the ones who mess you around the most. The painful parts of dating haven't changed. There are new technologies to communicate the pain, but the pain is the same.'

Danny asked about the worst dates and despite the Ecstasy in his system Matt answered seriously. 'Some people when I tell them I'm living with HIV, they walk straight out the door. Some claim they're fine and I never hear from them again.'

Back in his twenties Danny was prone to trade boundaries for affection, particularly when he was into a guy and they asked not to use a condom, Danny agreeing to please them, hoping they might stick around. Until he met Luis, he had chanced his way through the AIDS crisis, alive by a fluke. So many outside forces had nudged Danny and Luis together, it was hard to know whether these historical forces had been as important as their individual chemistry. Back then, they were exactly what the other needed. By asking him to marry him – the very question expressing a change of context – Danny was asking if they were what the other needed now. Perhaps it was true that every relationship, gay or straight, married or not, needed to regenerate after twenty years.

Sharing their most private stories Danny dusted off some of his favourite relationship quandaries, asking if Matt believed in the theory of love where there was one perfect person out there in the world – a soulmate waiting to be found. Matt shook his head.

'I've dated a lot. Many of those guys could have been great in different ways if they had stuck around. The *one* is the guy who *stays*. The *one* is the guy who builds something special with you. The more you build the more they become the one.'

Looking out over the city, Danny said, 'I couldn't go back to living without love. Sure, I could get *by* for a time. I'm not scared of being alone. Not like I was when I was young. But sharing the world with someone is better.'

Matt qualified the statement.

'Sharing the world with the wrong person is worse, my wards are full of patients with abusive partners. But sharing the world with the right person, I agree, that's the secret. Not really a secret. The secret that everyone knows.'

Their conversation was interrupted by a raggedy train of party guests clumsily climbing onto the roof. Tiles clattered to the street to the hilarity of some and outrage of others. Responsible neighbours began bellowing from open windows and threatening to call the police. Meanwhile, up on the chimney stacks, Danny and Matt judged it an opportune moment to swallow a second Ecstasy pill. Their fellow party guests began a countdown to midnight only to mistime it, forced to wait another sixteen seconds before Big Ben chimed and the fireworks erupted over the Thames.

It was the new year, the year Danny was set to marry, and here he was balancing on a rooftop, about to be arrested, high on Ecstasy with his arm around a handsome, emotionally available man who was not his fiancé. No chapter covered this scenario in any of the marriage guidebooks. Realizing he had not checked his phone for several hours he reached into his pocket, pulling it free, struggling to focus on the screen. He saw messages from his parents, Sophie, Jasper, various friends and colleagues but nothing from Luis. In that instant he was tempted to throw the phone as far as he could, to let it fly in a perfect parabola before it shattered on the street below. But the handset was new, he couldn't afford to replace it, and it might hit a passer-by. He slipped the phone back into his pocket, turning to Matt who had been watching him the whole time, with his back to a sky full of fireworks, indifferent to the glittering gold and silver streams.

'Happy New Year.'

And then they kissed.

# Chapter Thirty-Three

## *Holding Hands*

The police arrived. There was a scramble from the rooftop. The house party was broken up; guests scattered and somehow Danny ended up in a club. Nestled under the railway arches, the nightclub was a warren of brick-walled rooms packed to capacity, so full of guys that at times Danny wasn't moving of his own volition but as part of a collective held together by sound vibrations and sweat. He last went clubbing a decade ago and was surprised by the range of ages, including a muscular older man in his seventies wearing plastic sunglasses and decorated with neon beads like the high priest of this rave. As a young man Danny had never paid attention to the older guys before; they were invisible to him, as he was invisible to younger guys today.

Once inside, Danny and Matt were inseparable, sipping

from a shared bottle of mineral water and confronting each bizarre encounter with a mutual sense of delight. Most presumed they were a couple with passers-by commenting, 'You two are beautiful together.'

Danny was struck by the observation, curious whether it was merely a kind remark, part of the exuberance of the night. Luis and Danny had always enjoyed an intense physical connection in private, but they were reserved in public, an old-fashioned propriety originating from the fact that when they started dating public displays of affection risked ridicule and abuse. Merely standing side by side they had been shouted at by boisterous groups outside bars and once an empty can had been hurled from a passing car. Was it an accident, Luis had debated afterwards, thoughtless people threw rubbish from their cars, while Danny was in no doubt it was targeted, exasperated by Luis's denial. Those experiences early in their relationship were not easy to shake off. Danny and Luis lived together, slept together, shopped together, travelled together but never walked hand in hand. Danny could still remember the very first time he had seen a gay couple walking hand in hand, outside the National Theatre, their heads tilted towards the sky, not making eye contact with passers-by but resolutely holding hands like that was the whole point of them going for a walk. In this club there was no self-consciousness between Matt and himself. As Danny longed for such a thing to be possible in the world outside the club he wondered if it had become possible and he and Luis had simply missed the moment of change. At heart, that's what this wedding was – a chance for the pair of them to update, to become modern, ironically by embracing a tradition as old as any. What was a wedding, except an opportunity to hold hands and kiss, in front of a room full of people who would applaud or cry with happiness?

At the end of the night Danny and Matt retreated from the intensity of the club floor, standing on the outdoor terrace among plastic palm trees – the last remnants of Club Tropicana décor. They shared a spliff as a flag of surrender, a smoke signal to the universe that they had partied enough. With the Ecstasy fading they chose not to chase after the giddy pleasures of their initial high. One of the benefits of being older was knowing when to call it quits. On the dance floor Danny had taken off the cashmere sweater, pushing it into the back of his jeans, and several times it had fallen loose, trampled upon before it could be rescued. Examining it under a light he saw how stained it was with the ungodly slick of the club floor.

'It belongs to Luis.'

Rejecting the symbolism, Matt shook his head.

'Everyone kisses on pills. Everyone kisses on New Year's. It doesn't mean anything. And I say that as someone who would love for it to mean something. Danny, promise me that tomorrow you won't get sad. That's the opposite of why I invited you out.'

With defiance, Danny declared, 'I'm done with sad.'

A stranger standing nearby high-fived Danny.

'I'm done with sad too, baby.'

As the sky changed from black to bruised blue Danny recalled the sky on the very first night he spent with Luis. His mood was about to crash when Matt locked his arm through his and suggested breakfast. He wanted a full English with bacon, beans and fried eggs but Danny put forward another idea.

'There was a falafel place near Hungerford Bridge. I was drunk one night, at my lowest, with nowhere to sleep, no job, no money, no love – I've never tasted anything so good. Life-affirming. But I could never find the place again.'

Matt accepted the challenge.

They left the club and walked along the river, passing teams of workers collecting the smashed bottles and crumpled cans from the celebrations last night, men wearing heavy jackets and woolly hats while the pair of them sauntered past, scantily clad, arms wrapped around each other's shoulders. Danny half expected a glare or a slur to be muttered, but none of them cared. The world really had changed, he thought. Arriving at Hungerford Bridge Danny broke off, looking into the currents swirling around the bridge's pillars. Since the last time he had stood here, decades ago, the Samaritans had added a plaque with a telephone number for anyone needing help.

Wandering for a time, they eventually found the kiosk behind the Queen Elizabeth Hall, near Waterloo Station. 'Semoorg Falafel' was doing a brisk trade with New Year's Eve clubbers, customers with eyes weeping glitter, tangled hair and smudged make-up. None of them worried about their appearance as they braved the fluorescent lights to buy hot pittas loaded with beef tomatoes and creamy tahini dressing. Perhaps all those years ago Danny had bought food here, a place that only manifested itself when you took yourself to the brink.

Danny and Matt returned to the river and ate their pittas on the steps down to the water while sipping cans of fiery Jamaican ginger ale and watching the weak winter sunrise. Matt declared, 'This year I'm going to fall in love.'

Taking out his phone, Danny said, 'I might need to join you in that search.'

Danny focused on his screen and saw the missed messages from Luis, wishing him Happy New Year and telling him he was ready to come home.

# Chapter Thirty-Four

## *Luis's Return*

A few days later Danny was at home tidying up when the phone rang. It was Luis. The marriage proposal had been volcanic, as destructive as it was creative. It was time to discover if the lava had hardened into two islands or one. Danny turned the radio off, sat down and answered the call.

'Hello, Luis.'

Luis was back in London after marking the traditional religious holiday of *Día de los Reyes Magos* with school friends in Madrid. Danny tried to recall who Luis's school friends might be as if he were about to be tested and the fate of the wedding would depend upon remembering at least two names. Luis asked, 'Are you free for dinner?'

It sounded like they were going on a first date, not far from the truth. Danny suppressed the urge to joke about checking his diary. He was no longer sure how his jokes would land. Luis might interpret the comment literally, imagining that he had bought a diary for the first time in his life. Better to be matter of fact, Danny thought, which was a lot of thought to give to the reply, 'Yes, I'm free.'

Luis suggested that they meet in a restaurant rather than at home. Regretting the question immediately, Danny blurted out, 'Is it still our home?'

Luis said it would be better if they talked face to face and Danny agreed.

The phone conversation lasted three minutes and thirty-three seconds, a set of numbers so neat and tidy they seemed to have been trimmed with a knife. Recently Danny had developed a habit of muttering uplifting remarks to himself, becoming his own cheerleader. He placed a hand on his heart to steady an irregular beat and declared, 'Hold it together, pal.'

A short time later he received a text message from Luis suggesting dinner on Friday at a Scandinavian restaurant in Soho. Danny had never heard of the place. Online, he studied the gallery of images. It was a recent opening, with no memories or associations. Neutral ground. The dining space was open with no partitioned booths. Danny concluded that Luis wanted the company of other diners to moderate their emotions, the inverse logic of choosing an engagement location, which made sense if you were intending to undo a proposal. Instead of seclusion, a crowd. Instead of presenting a ring, a ring would be returned.

Danny told no one the news. He didn't want his mind cluttered with well-meaning opinions. They would meet as equals – two explorers returning from separate adventures. At their first Soho meeting, when Luis had worn smart attire with the keys to a penthouse apartment, Danny had treated him as fully formed, an idealized man who rarely lost control, drank in moderation, never touched drugs, worked to excess – a provider. By contrast, he was the young one who needed improvement. Danny strove to be healthier, sexier, smarter – to read more books and bake better cakes. He had never stopped to wonder whether, in fact, Luis was the more incomplete.

On Thursday evening, the night before the dinner, Danny carefully laid out his outfit, opting for sombre clothes including a white shirt from Reiss, a black sweater and grey trousers, dialling back the eccentricity without trying to present himself as a different man. Except he was different and he was sure Luis would be too. He shaved carefully and slept soundly. Late Friday afternoon he left the hospital and returned home to shower and change. Despite it being bitterly cold, he decided to walk into Soho, as he had done the night they first met. In Chinatown he browsed the set menus, worried he might arrive red-faced. Continuing onwards, he found the small restaurant. He was ten minutes early. Rather than circle the block he walked straight in.

There was an open-plan kitchen with polished steel shelves filled with glass jars of unusual spices and foraged herbs. In the main dining area every table was occupied, each decorated with a single sprig of unfurled forest fern, the only curve in a room of straight edges. Luis was seated at a table by the window, watching the passers-by, strategically placed for the first glimpse of Danny. Except Danny had avoided walking past the windows for exactly this reason. Luis's hair was longer, a mass of foppish curls. Danny marvelled at the sight of Luis, as if they were a couple who had spent twenty years corresponding and this was their first time meeting in person. His clothes were new – not lawyer sharp or city-chic, no shirts, ties or suits. They were softer, an embroidered patterned cardigan, straw-yellow with winter wool trousers, the fashion of an Alpine farmer. No longer shorthand handsome, Danny thought, but profoundly, deeply so.

Sensing Danny's arrival Luis turned to him and stood up. Neither man moved for a moment, as if the meeting had been a surprise, and then Danny approached and they hugged, holding on to each other for ten seconds then twenty until it became a minute or more and it seemed that they might never let go. Danny had wondered how they would greet each other, with a handshake or a hug or a nod of the head. In person their bodies knew the answer – to bring themselves as close as possible for as long as possible. In a break with their past Luis seemed oblivious to the spectacle of their public affection and it was Danny who subtly signalled they should end the hug not because he wasn't enjoying it but because he was desperate to hear what Luis had to say. Though he had imagined a wide variety of emotions at their reunion, mostly he felt relief. This was love, he thought. Not the remnants of it, the embers of a once-bright fire. Whatever else happened tonight, whatever was said or decided, he told himself to hold on to this instinctual reaction. There had been, still was, and always would be, the strongest of bonds between them.

As they sat down Danny was smiling in part because he was happy after the hug but also to reaffirm that he wasn't here to argue or lay down a litany of grievances. No longer was he bothered about the 'normal' process of engagements. He was grateful they were doing this their way, whatever their way might be. Around Luis's neck hung the small silver crucifix which had once belonged to his grandfather. He had never worn it before, keeping it in his drawer, only occasionally taking it out when he prayed. He was still wearing his engagement ring and the two items of jewellery matched well together.

The waiter approached, a thin man with pale skin and small blue tattoos spotted across his veined forearms. He asked for their drink order and though Danny had promised himself that he wouldn't drink alcohol, on a whim he changed his mind. Glancing at the menu his eyes chanced on a Nordic martini served with aquavit and angelica root. With not a clue what these flavours amounted to, he ordered one. Luis stuck to sparkling water. Once the waiter left Luis asked, 'Should I speak first?'

Danny nodded, of course, it was Luis's turn to talk, suggesting that they wait for the drink to be delivered so they wouldn't be interrupted. Making small talk that was as rich with meaning as anything grand they might say, Danny complimented Luis's cardigan. Luis glanced down at it.

'There was snow one day in Madrid.'

Danny tried to picture the scene. As a couple they had only visited the city once. It had been the autumn. During that long weekend Danny had been curious at how introverted Luis seemed, avoiding the gay quarter, the bars and the clubs, acting more like a tourist, visiting the galleries and museums, and meeting none of Luis's friends who, he had explained, were spread across Europe.

The waiter arrived with a chilled glass shaped like an upside-down cathedral bell. He flipped out a small notepad to take their food order. Danny asked for more time, adding that they would signal when they were ready. The waiter looked at them, assessing the encounter. Of course, he said. After he left, Danny took a sip of his martini, noticing that the usual olive had been replaced with a cloudberry. How pleasing and pretty it was, the table setting, the forest fern and Luis. He wished he could stay in this moment before anything irreversible was said. How stupid he had been to rush out of their hug. The taste of the martini was inexplicable, neither pleasant nor unpleasant, simply strong and cold as though he had ordered a chilled shot of fortitude. He put the glass down, placing his palms flat on the table in the manner of a magician midway through a card trick demonstrating that there was nothing in his hands and nothing up his sleeves.

Accepting his cue, Luis began by stating that he had arranged a period of extended leave from work, an unprecedented request in his long career. Since arriving in London Luis's singular goal was to be made partner at a top law firm. Achieving this position had taken on a mythic significance in his mind. It would prove that coming out hadn't limited his ambitions – that he had overcome the obstacle of his sexuality. On the threshold of this goal, to take two months off would appear to his colleagues to be the worst of weaknesses – vulnerability and sentimentality. We always knew it about him, they would claim, with a knowing glance. He could only *appear* to be like one of us, but never truly *be* one of us. Skimming over the severity of these consequences, Luis explained that he didn't have a clear plan for his time in Spain beyond reconnecting with his past but, once there, he had set out on a tour of his country, visiting the towns he had always wanted to visit but never found the time, starting at El Escorial, close to Madrid, before travelling by train to Ávila, Salamanca, Zamora, La Coruña, Lugo and León. The list sounded so specific that Danny asked about it and Luis was pleased at the question.

'Out of nowhere, I remembered an obscure fact about the playwright Federico Lorca. I must have read it at school. How he went on a tour of Spain during his formative years. I decided to follow in Federico's footsteps, visiting the same sequence of towns. I admit, it is a little late for my formative years, but that is the nature of our story, Danny – we are doing these things out of time?'

There had always been an intrepid quality about Luis. There was a restlessness in his soul that could only be soothed by a constant stream of accomplishments, either professional or personal, even his holidays needed summits, yet this tour seemed different, following in the steps of a gay playwright, someone whose works were encoded as queer, because Lorca could not write openly at the time, using repressed female sexuality as a proxy for his own.

Luis said, 'I stayed in simple guest houses. I would wake up early, eat a breakfast of bread and cheese, then walk through every square and down every avenue. I visited museums, parks, galleries and markets. At each church I would stop, light a candle and pray. At night I'd find the oldest restaurant in town. I never looked at a menu. I'd ask for whatever the chef considered to be their best dish. For weeks, that was how I lived. A pilgrim in my own country.'

Briefly Danny tried to imagine what it would have been like to go on this trip together before supposing that Luis didn't want to play the role of a guide. He wasn't showing off his homeland, he was rediscovering it – searching not for a place on a map but somewhere inside of himself.

Luis observed, 'My Spanish sounds strange to other native speakers. Stiff. Like I learned it from a dictionary. A few asked where I was born, supposing I was born abroad.'

Luis indicated the Nordic martini.

'May I?'

As though it were a chess piece, a rook, Danny slid it across the tabletop. Luis took a sip, giving no reaction to the combination of flavours before returning the glass to Danny's side.

'I met many interesting people along the way. There was a literature professor at Salamanca University. He had recently been travelling through South America on a sabbatical in much the same way as I was travelling through Spain. He told me a story. And I saw myself in it. You know how it can be with stories? You hear them, and you want to stop, stand up and tell everyone that character is you.'

At this point Luis paused.

'I know you have a lot of questions, Danny, and I'm taking the scenic route.'

*What a cute phrase*, Danny thought, appreciating that Luis didn't want to sound lawyerly and business-like, but lyrical and loose. He leaned forward, placing his hand on top of Luis's.

'Tell me anything you want, any way you want to.'

The truth was that Danny was quite delighted by the way Luis was talking. After speaking Spanish for such an extended period Luis's voice had changed, the way he spoke English sounded faster and more fluid, the words rolling into each other rather than standing on their own. Danny had always loved the sound of Luis's voice, but now even more so.

'The professor was visiting a town called Cali, in Colombia, where there's a festival called the *Cabalgata* which derives from the verb *cabalgar* – "to ride". Residents bring their horses onto the street. Since the land around Cali is mountainous with farms, many people own horses, not only the rich. The professor—'

Danny dared to interrupt, 'What was his name?'

Luis nodded at the question, acknowledging there was an intimacy between them.

'His name was André. He was staying with relatives who loaned him one of their horses in order that he could experience the carnival as a participant rather than as a spectator.

On the day of the festival, he was one among many thousands of riders. And it's a carnival, not a parade. He was drinking *viche*, a spirit brewed from sugar cane, mixed with fresh mango juice or pineapple pulp, sweet and strong, and in the sun, you're drunk in an instant.'

Danny quipped, 'How about we order two?'

Luis nodded.

'You know, when I was young, I used to ride horses. Wild ones, which roamed the countryside outside of town.'

Danny had no idea. He pictured young Luis riding horses in the wild.

'My grandfather taught me. We would head into the countryside. He would catch them, and I would ride them. He said I had a gift. They were always calm around me. I was never scared. I miss that young man, without fear.'

Conversations had always been this way between Danny and Luis, tangents and diversions, sometimes so many the pair forgot the initial subject of their conversation. Danny would happily have talked about wild horses and sugar cane for the rest of the evening, but he gently returned Luis to his original point.

'So – this literature professor who I've never met was drinking *viche*, a drink I've never heard of, in a town I've never visited.'

Luis smiled at the summary.

'By late afternoon André was drunk. Of course, no one

organizing the festival was concerned about safety. And by the evening André was so drunk he was in danger of falling off his horse. To stop this from happening he slumped forward and wrapped his arms tight around the horse's neck, which startled the animal. The horse broke into a gallop. All André could do was hold on to the mane. The horse bolted through the town, through streets André had never seen. It ran and ran until eventually, exhausted, the horse came to a stop and André slowly sat up, with no idea where he was. There were three young kids staring at him from a window, laughing at him.'

Luis tapped the table.

'That is me, Danny, clinging to a career, galloping faster and faster, trying not to fall with no idea where I was going or why. When you proposed to me – I stopped. And I looked around. I asked myself, where am I? What am I doing? Who am I?'

Danny asked, 'What was your answer?'

Luis sighed. 'You were right to say that part of me has remained in the closet. At first, I bristled at the idea that I wasn't "gay enough". That I hadn't marched enough or signed enough petitions. But I realized that wasn't what you meant. I haven't been myself enough. I haven't given you all of myself because I didn't have all of myself to give. I am a well-crafted presentation of a man because I was told I could never be a real one.'

The orange cloudberry sitting in the clear spirits of Danny's glass recalled to his mind the brightly painted hammers in glass boxes on trains or the tube. *Break in an Emergency.* Using his fork he fished the berry free, putting it in his mouth. And waited.

Luis said, 'I quit my job.'

Danny felt a sense of panic, that instead of creating something beautiful with his proposal, he had broken everything, including Luis himself.

'Luis, I never wanted you to quit your job. It was never a choice between us or your career.'

Luis agreed.

'That's not what this is. I was a man for other people. I've always been a man for other people. But to marry someone, you need to offer yourself. You cannot do that if you don't know who you are.'

Having listened for almost thirty minutes, Danny sat up straight and explained, 'Luis, before we go any further there's something I need to tell you. On New Year's Eve I kissed Matt. The nurse. From the Olympics. There was a party. We were high. I was lonely and I fucked up.'

Luis stared at the fern on their table.

'This is the question, no? Do we change together or change apart? Do we change with each other or with someone else?'

Danny managed to ask, 'What's your answer?'

Luis mused. 'I've spent this time away thinking how much I want to change my life. But the only part I don't want to change is you.'

Danny had done well so far. He had been stoic and measured but at hearing this he wept. Luis moved his chair around the table, wiping away his tears.

'Danny, you've always been this way. You understand feelings by acting on them. You didn't ask if I loved you – you asked if I wanted to live with you. You didn't say that you were unhappy – you suggested a garden. You didn't point out something is missing from our lives – you proposed.'

At this inopportune moment the waiter returned.

'I'm sorry for interrupting but the kitchen will be closing soon so I need to take your order.'

Danny didn't bother hiding his tears. Copying Luis's method in Spain he said, 'Why don't you choose for us? The chef's best dish?'

To lighten the mood, Luis asked for two glasses of *viche*. The waiter had never heard of the spirit and so, improvising, Luis suggested light rum as a substitute spirit, mixed with pineapple juice. Once the waiter left, Danny asked, 'What now?'

Luis made a proposal of his own, as consequential as the one Danny had attempted.

'How about we try to change together? I don't know if it's possible, but I wanted to see if you would be open to the idea. My entire life I've been translating myself. Growing up, I was translating myself into a straight man. Respected and respectable. When that fell apart, I moved to London and began translating myself into a career man. I don't want to be in translation anymore. I'm missing part of myself. And I can't find it here. I want to go home, Danny. If we had been husband and wife, the chances are we would've combined our lives from the beginning, our families and cultures. Instead, we've been exiles in London in our different ways. We shared our loneliness and isolation. It's time we shared everything which is, I believe, what you were asking me to do when you proposed.'

At this point Danny reached into his pocket and took out the First World War compass – Luis's Christmas present. He wasn't sure why he had brought it with him to the restaurant or why at this juncture in the conversation he took it from his pocket. He placed it on the centre of the table and the two of them watched the needle find north.

'I bought it for us. To help us find the way.'

Danny had promised himself that he wouldn't drink or cry and now having broken both promises he was unable to hold back the tears.

'Would it be easier to say this is the end? To raise a glass to all the great times we've had together, to be thankful for them, to say that I love you, I'll always love you, and go our separate ways?'

Luis turned the question over.

'That might be the outcome, yes. But, Danny, I'm suggesting that we build a new life and the only person I've ever built a life with is you. Could we do it again? I don't know.'

Though Danny desperately wanted to say yes, he found himself asking, 'Tell me, deep down, that this isn't an elaborate way of breaking up and that after twenty years it's too painful for either one of us to say it's over. I ask you to marry me. And you ask me to move to Spain. Maybe we're both saying the same thing – that it's over?'

In an unplanned moment, prompted by the gift of the compass, Luis took off his grandfather's silver necklace and placed it around Danny's neck. A proposal answered with a proposal. A platinum ring with a silver necklace. And neither of them knew what to say next.

Part Four

# Spring

# Chapter Thirty-Five

## *A Perfect Man*

Luis moved back in, living with Danny in the home they made together while readying it for sale. As a couple, they had contributed different amounts to the initial deposit according to their means. Regardless, Luis suggested they share the profit equally. If they managed to find a path through, they would pool their money into somewhere new. After the garden party last summer, it had been Danny's idea to sell the apartment and move, longing for a garden of their own. Yet now that the plans were in motion, he was haunted by memories of himself as a homeless young man who once stored his possessions in a left-luggage locker in Victoria Station while he slept on a park bench in Embankment Gardens.

The estate agent appraising their apartment was no older

than thirty, dressed in a cobalt-blue flannel suit with a silver tie and polished leather shoes. Fifteen years their junior, he addressed them as 'lads' as he declared their home would be perfect for a single man trying to impress a lady, or a recently married couple before they bought their first family home. It was strange, listening to the agent rewrite the story of their apartment according to a traditional life-sequence – a bus stop of a home on the road towards a family. Luis and Danny looked at each other. Catching their glances and sensing there were ripples of communication he didn't understand, the agent hastily added that the place could also work for an older bachelor type. Bringing the conversation to a close Danny asked when they should consider listing. The agent said, 'This summer will be strong. International buyers are returning. London is red-hot after the Olympics. The recession will be in the rear-view mirror. We're expecting price rises of eight per cent. Lads, you've done a great job. Trust me, we'll be able to sell it in no time. And considering how long ago you bought it you're set to make a tidy profit. Where are you guys moving to? Somewhere bigger?'

Their relationship entered an experimental phase with Danny exploring the possibility of emigrating, a man who had never lived abroad or ever seriously given thought to doing so. Considering his partner was Spanish it was a failure of imagination. Luis's proposal was not to create a

Spanish approximation of their London life but to create a new life together – one Danny could neither describe nor envision. The future appeared blank, except for one guiding point – home had never been the apartment; home had always been Luis.

Compared to the emotional complexities of relocating the practicalities were straightforward. Even though they weren't married, Danny didn't need to apply for residency or a visa and his skills as a nurse would be in demand. He would require competence in Spanish if he were to be employed in the 'Sistema Nacional de Salud' – the public health care system. However, his seniority and pay scale wouldn't transfer over. He would be starting at a lower rung and confined to the private sector until his language skills improved. When he floated the idea to his colleagues their reactions were mixed. They had been delighted by the news of his wedding. Many were attending. But that wedding now depended on losing a cherished member of the team. He would be giving up years of hard-won progression at a hospital where he was respected, to begin again in a place where he would be unknown. Part of what made him a great nurse was his ability to befriend patients and until his Spanish was fluent, he would struggle to form the same bonds, performing the mechanical tasks of a nurse without the magic of human connections. Luis had not only learned English perfectly, he had also immersed himself in the cultural references, something Danny would need to mirror. Where once there had been books on the monarchy and the Beatles, the bedside table now held books on Goya, Lorca and the Spanish Civil War.

The first test would come in March when they would travel to Spain, to the southern region of Andalucía, spending time in Seville and Cádiz where Luis was born and raised. As a couple they had never visited Andalucía together. Until this winter, Luis had only returned once to attend his grandfather's funeral. At the time he argued that bringing a boyfriend would be a provocation, upsetting his relatives. It was during the early years of their relationship and Danny accepted his exclusion, accustomed to the fact that there would always be places in the world where they were not welcome together. Yet looking back, it was not society excluding him. It was Luis. He had built a wall around his past.

Danny began taking Spanish lessons. Each evening he and Luis spent an hour or so at the kitchen table with notebooks and verb tables. Not since school had he studied a foreign language, an experience he found excruciating, hating the sound of his own voice, laughed at in class, not only when he mispronounced words in French but when he sounded camp in English, his native tongue sounding foreign – the essence of his voice seeming to be masculinity mispronounced. In contrast, Luis was an excellent teacher, patient and thorough, advising him not to worry about his accent, pointing out that some of the United Nations delegates spoke with a strong accent. Accents were story. Danny's Spanish accent was the story of a man reshaping his life for love. One evening their Spanish lesson centred on descriptions of a person's romantic status, the words for 'married', 'husband', 'partner', 'boyfriend' and 'engagement'. Midway through the lesson Luis lost his train of thought. When he regained his composure he said, 'This is not the first time I've been engaged.'

The piece of news was dropped into the lesson as if it was merely a practice sentence for Danny to translate.

Danny wrote down the word – *comprometido* – pressing the nib of the pen so hard on the paper the letters became grooves. In the adjacent column he wrote the incorrect translation – 'compromised'. He put the pen down and fetched a glass of water, asking, 'Who was she?'

Luis described a young woman called Isabella. Even though he didn't say she was beautiful, Danny pictured her so. Born in Cádiz, she was the same age as Luis and had attended the same school. Her passion was painting. She would paint people at work, such as the butcher, the florist or a man selling lottery tickets. As a couple, they were attractive and popular. Luis was academic, she was creative. For Danny coming out merely confirmed everyone's suspicions and justified their cruel jokes. But for Luis it had been a fall from grace and a loss of status. As Luis spoke about Isabella his voice broke. He had loved this woman, Danny realized.

'How long were you together?'

Acknowledging the seriousness of the relationship Luis paused before replying, 'Six years.'

They were school sweethearts. Like in the movies. After graduating from university, Luis proposed. At the proper time, Danny thought, the correct time, the perfect time, with their whole life ahead of them.

'How did you do it? Propose, I mean? How did you propose to her?'

Luis looked upwards.

'Does it matter?'

Danny had spent so long thinking about the process he was now curious about every engagement, even ones that caused him pain.

'It might.'

Luis reluctantly recalled the scene.

'It was in the summer. At night. We were on the beach beside Castillo de Santa Catalina in Cádiz. The ring belonged to my grandmother. She left it to me in her will. Along with a letter hoping I would give it to Isabella one day.'

Danny asked, 'Did you go down on one knee?'

Luis nodded.

'Yes, I went down on one knee.'

It was as traditional a proposal as could be imagined. Danny marvelled at the scene.

'You put the ring on her finger, didn't you? I fucked that part up. But you snatched the box from my hands. What could I do? Snatch it back? Now that I think about it, did you take it from me because it felt wrong?'

Luis was quiet for a time and then answered, 'Yes, it felt wrong. In my gut. I took the box away from you, because I was trying to stop it from happening.'

Finally, Danny understood what had happened in the Highlands. He could play back the proposal, making sense of the hesitations and expressions.

Rejoining Luis at the table, Danny asked how long the engagement to Isabella lasted. Luis said it was only for one summer. Trying to guess why it might have ended, Danny wondered if this was the point at which Luis came out.

'Danny, I never came out. Not in the way you mean. During my time with Isabella there were hook-ups with guys. Behind the sand dunes. In the public toilets. I thought to myself, I can keep this side of me out of sight. I need occasional relief. That's all. I can't build my life around it. Those encounters were about sex and nothing more. I never asked for names. I never told them my name. I searched for visitors and tourists who would leave town after a few days – men who would disappear. Despite my precautions it was a small town. Someone told someone who told someone else. After the engagement was announced there was a party.'

In a quiet voice Danny amended the word.

'An engagement party.'

Luis accepted the point, remembering that he had opposed one for the two of them.

'It wasn't planned. We didn't rent a bar, send out invitations or spend any money. Her parents were happy for us. They opened some wine. They rang some friends, shared the news. It happened naturally.'

Danny repeated the phrase.

'Naturally.'

Luis accepted his mistake – his words revealing the depth of his internalized self-loathing.

'A few days later Isabella was taken aside and told not to marry me. That I was not right in the head. That I was a man who had sex with men. That our marriage would end in misery, disease and tragedy. For a week she was distant. I asked her to tell me what was wrong. She confronted me.'

Danny guessed, 'And you denied it?'

Luis nodded. 'Yes, I denied it. I said someone was trying to destroy me because they were jealous. I begged her to stay with me. I was on my knees, snot coming out of my nose, promising to do anything, claiming I would never even look at another man, assuring her it was a grubby part of me that I could suffocate and bury. I would be the best husband she could possibly desire, a perfect man, I would work harder than any man on earth, I would adore her, care for her, if she married me. It was one of the lowest moments in my life. I was a condemned man pleading for a stay of execution. I knew if she broke it off I would be destroyed. Everyone would want to know why the engagement had ended when we were the perfect couple. Another woman? That would be one thing. But men? In the bathroom and on the beaches? That would be the end of me.'

Danny was amazed.

'You asked her to live your lie?'

Luis was back in that moment again, hearing her reply, remembering the anguish of begging, the loss of dignity.

'She refused. If I wanted to be blind that was my decision. But she was an artist. The most important sensibility in an artist is honesty. She was hopelessly idealistic, I told her. About art. About love. But she would not budge. She was sure that the foundation of any marriage is truth. She spoke about the sadness she had seen in me. The loneliness even when we were together. If we married, if she overlooked the truth, she would be forever wondering what was in my mind. So, it ended. The town found out. I was called names as I walked down the street.'

Listening to Luis, a question occurred to Danny.

'Who told Isabella?'

Luis stood up, leaving the table and standing in the darkness.

'My father.'

At this mention of his father Luis's voice changed. There was fury in it, new to Danny's ear. Luis put a hand on the windowpane.

'My dad was a drunk, charming in the evenings with a glass of wine in his hand, savage in the morning when the wine wore off. If he thought he could impress you he put on a show. If you doubted him, he was vicious. It always surprised me when I was learning English that people associate the word "vicious" with gay men. In my life no one was more vicious than my father. If challenged about why he needed to borrow money or why he didn't come home last night he would attack you as though you were questioning his existence, which you were, because he lived inside his lies. To strangers he would perform, playing the role of a man on the cusp of achieving great things, fame and riches were always one sunrise away. With my mother and me, he would bully and belittle us because we knew the truth, that he was a small man. Looking back, I think he enjoyed his affairs less for the sex and more for the audience of women who didn't know him. During those one-night stands he could be anyone. When he returned home he was a failure and he hated us for seeing the real him.'

In all their time together Luis had never spoken with such contempt for anyone. That he and his father were estranged,

Danny knew. However, it was hard to fathom that his father, a man preoccupied with masculinity, had outed his own son.

'Why would he out you?'

Luis moved out of the darkness, returning to the table. It took an effort for Danny not to recoil from his passions.

'He was a fraud. It was hell to him that I knew it. When he had the chance to tell everyone that I was the worse fraud, he took it. It made him seem less of one. He was a real man. I was the fake one. Everyone had thought he was the bad man but now he seemed wholesome in comparison. He ruined me in the eyes of many in the town, in the eyes of my grandfather and in the eyes of the priest set to marry me.'

As fast as it had been summoned, Luis's anger dissipated, replaced with sadness. He sat down.

'And my mother? She said that she would rather I had died so that she could remember the boy I had been. In a way I did die. My life as I knew it ended.'

Danny considered.

'Did you confront your dad?'

Luis nodded.

'It was the last time we spoke. I told him that he wasn't my father. He told me I wasn't his son. We agreed on that much at least.'

That night neither of them slept. Marriage for Danny had been an idyllic pasture he had intended to walk through arm in arm with Luis. But to Luis, marriage was a battleground filled with the wreckage of betrayals, a place he had vowed never to return to. In the morning Danny suggested a walk. The pair of them meandered through the gardens of the Imperial War Museum without purpose or direction. Rhododendrons and camellias were beginning to bloom and crocuses were breaking through the grass. Eventually Danny asked why Luis had never told him the truth.

'It was too demeaning. We never spoke about marriage when we met. It wasn't a possibility, so it never came up until the laws around civil partnership were brought in. At that point, it felt so long ago. I didn't know how you'd react.'

Danny said, 'You did know. That's why you never mentioned it. Because it's so obviously the life you wanted. You didn't give it up, Luis. It was stolen from you. And you've never got over it. Part of your heart is still on that beach.'

Luis agreed.

'That's why we need to go back. I accepted the truth at that time. Marriage was never meant for people like me.'

Danny adjusted the phrase.

'For people like us.'

At the museum café Luis and Danny sat in the corner. Though they had bought breakfast rolls, neither of them touched their food. Sipping his bitter black coffee, Danny said, 'I've spent our entire relationship wondering if I was good enough for you. The truth is that's all I was – good enough.'

Upset, Luis turned the point around.

'No, I've never thought of you in those terms. But I did think of myself that way. And as I sit here, all I'm wondering is whether I'm good enough for you.'

# Chapter Thirty-Six

## *Matthew Roche & Christopher Cramp*

Danny and Luis sat down with Jasper at his Covent Garden office to decide whether to amend or cancel their wedding plans. Throughout his life Danny had suffered from bouts of anxiety that he was letting people down, parents, friends, colleagues, because at some point during childhood he accepted that letting people down was not an event or an incident – it was his identity. Being gay was a letdown from being straight. He had spent his adulthood trying to uproot that definition, applying rationality and positivity. Nonetheless, minor failures were often indistinguishable from major ones, since they reaffirmed the same underlying belief. One of the loftier hopes from last summer was that a wedding would free him from this recurring sensation. Instead, the engagement now presented an opportunity to let down everyone in his life at the same time in the most public way possible.

In the meeting Jasper kept his notebook closed, adopting a more measured and formal tone that Danny found both understandable and upsetting. After hearing Luis talk about his desire for the wedding to be a new beginning rather than an affirmation of the past, Jasper eased into the conversation. The fact that Luis had skipped their first meeting now made sense. Jasper asked Luis the questions he would've asked back then – what marriage meant to him, including memories from his childhood. Luis was able to answer openly.

'My family would attend almost every wedding in town. Even if we only knew the couple a little. They were one of the few occasions my parents wouldn't fight. At weddings a stranger might mistake them for being in love. Back at home, when the only person watching was me – my parents would fight again, and I always wondered why they couldn't behave like they did during the ceremony. There was one wedding in particular, when I was very young. It took place in the cathedral in Cádiz between two wealthy families. We sat at the back. I remember turning around when the bride entered. The sunlight was behind her veil. The air smelt of incense. Truly a union blessed by God. My dad hugged me tight, which was rare. Afterwards, at the reception, he told me that one day I would be married, and my wedding would be even bigger, and my bride would be even more beautiful. He boasted to the guests about my great future, telling everyone how clever I was, how successful my career would be and how splendid my wedding would be. He loved me, at that party, because everyone believed him.'

Jasper stood up and walked over to the window. He looked at the busy street below.

'Do either of you know about the first civil partnership registered in this country?'

They didn't. Jasper continued, 'The two men were Matthew Roche and Christopher Cramp. The venue was St Barnabas House Hospice in Worthing. The date was the 5th of December 2005. Eight years ago. There were fifteen guests. Matthew was in a wheelchair with a blanket over his legs, too weak to stand. For the ceremony, Christopher sat beside him wearing a yellow shirt. I wasn't there. I know these details only from the newspaper articles and photographs. At the end of the day the hospice staff put another bed in Matthew's room and Christopher slept beside him – that was their honeymoon, a night together in the hospice, their first and only night as legally recognized partners. The following day Matthew died of cancer. He had clung on to life long enough to be married to the man he loved. Why am I telling you this? Because these were the wedding stories we didn't have growing up. But we have them now. For years they've had cathedrals while we've had hospices and hospitals. While they have weddings, we have funerals. It's time to move on. This wedding can't be a farewell to your past. It can only be a celebration of your future.'

Jasper concluded, 'If you want to give up Black Rabbit Farm I can find another wedding to take the slot so you're not on the hook for the costs. But you need to decide today, in this room, not after the trip to Spain. Easter will be too late for anyone to make plans. And this isn't simply about the money; it's about whether that venue still feels true to the two of you.'

Luis remained silent, not wishing to intervene in this decision. Danny loved the farm with the herb garden, the threshing barn and the marriage forest.

Jasper pressed, 'Gentlemen, do we hold on to Black Rabbit Farm or give it up?'

Danny replied with a certainty that surprised everyone, 'Give it up.'

# Chapter Thirty-Seven

## *A Cautionary Tale*

When he heard the news about Danny's possible move to Spain Matt asked if they could meet up. Rather than a bar or a coffee shop, he offered a tour around his new place of work, a mental health hospital in West London where he had recently been transferred and promoted to consultant nurse. Danny supposed that Matt not only wanted to talk, he also wanted to show another side of his life away from the clubs and parties, to prove that he was a serious person with responsibilities, a man who cared for others and excelled at his work. That evening Danny told Luis about Matt's invitation. Luis thought for a time, aware that Matt might be presenting himself as an alternative.

'You should go.'

*

Northwick Park Hospital was a maze of low-rise seventies concrete buildings. Matt met him at the front gates where they hugged. The ward was secured with two sets of locked doors, one on the ground floor, the second upstairs at the end of a narrow corridor. Inside some of the patients sat on chairs, still and sick. Other patients paced the hall, their agitation so severe it was hard to imagine them ever being at peace. There were young men with crystal meth-induced psychosis. There were older men whose psychosis remained a mystery. Neither Danny nor Matt spoke much inside the ward. Danny grew self-conscious about the soles of his shoes squeaking on the linoleum floor. After the tour Danny breathed deeply, putting a hand on Matt's shoulder.

'How do you cope?'

Matt replied, 'Sometimes I don't.'

In Northwick Park, a mosaic of dog-walking lawns and five-a-side football pitches, they found a secluded spot under the branches of a horse chestnut tree. Danny, knowing hospital canteen food, had made his own sandwiches filled with spiced jackfruit and red cabbage slaw accompanied by two wedges of a home-baked carrot cake. Delighted by the offering Matt had brought a mauve hospital blanket, which he spread over the grass. Danny shared the sandwiches and they ate for a time before Matt said, 'It's been bothering me. The idea that you might see my life as a cautionary tale. A single guy in his late thirties, frittering away his weekends on drugs and dancing, punished for his promiscuity.'

Danny put a hand on his arm.

'Matt, that thought has never crossed my mind.'

But Matt continued, 'I don't care what most people think about me. But I care what you think. I'm not going to offer any opinion on whether you should move to Spain with Luis because only you can know. But I wanted to tell you this: I was in a relationship in my twenties and head over heels in love with the guy. I would've done anything for him. And I did. He asked if we could stop using protection. He said it would be more intimate. I agreed. That's when I contracted HIV, not when I was single, not when I was sleeping around. After I tested positive it was like a double diagnosis. My health and my judge of character. Here's the worst part. I stayed with him. For two more years. Because I was terrified of being on my own. After that relationship ended it was hard to trust anyone. Every time I went into the clinic to have a check-up I would fill out those questionnaires. One of the questions is – *have you ever agreed to anything in a sexual relationship which made you uncomfortable?* Every visit, I was flagged as at risk from domestic abuse. That's how I saw myself – as a weak man, too weak to be in love because the other person would always take advantage. Danny, I'm not trying to say this isn't the right move for you. I don't know Luis. I just want to make sure that you don't think of *me* as a cautionary tale.'

Danny replied, 'Matt, I promise, if I move to Spain, one of the hardest challenges will be leaving you behind.'

Content with this answer Matt lay down on the blanket resting his head on Danny's leg. Danny ran his fingers through Matt's hair, curious how the act of intimacy would feel. Matt closed his eyes. In the distance a group of kids began playing football. The sounds of their laughter drifted over and for once it didn't feel like they were laughing at them.

# Chapter Thirty-Eight

## *An Offer*

Ahead of the exploratory visit to Spain, Danny's parents arrived in London to meet Luis for the first time. Luis took charge of the evening, offering to prepare a variety of traditional Andalusian dishes. He had never cooked these for Danny, in the same way that he had never taken him to the south of Spain. It was trivial by comparison, but another wall was coming down. They spent Saturday morning buying produce from specialist traders at Borough Market near London Bridge including fresh sardines, Manzanilla olives, Payoyo cheese and Monastrell red wine. At home Danny set about baking a traditional *tarta de almendra* based on Luis's grandmother's recipe, made with lemon zest and grated cinnamon. As they worked side by side in the kitchen Luis wondered how Danny's parents would feel about their plan.

'As you make peace with your parents, I ask you to move abroad.'

Danny pointed out that his parents would see him more in Spain than they ever had in London and they would be happy for the chance to travel now that the Bude guest house was being run so well.

When Danny's parents arrived they both gave Luis a hug, not an awkward handshake but an embrace. The introduction was so warm everyone started laughing without knowing why it was so funny. After they settled down, Danny's mother glanced at her son, concerned tonight might be full of inadvertent wrong words or misjudged questions. Putting her at ease Danny kissed her on the cheek, while his dad quipped, 'We hear you wish to make an honest man out of our son.'

Luis replied, 'It's your son who made an honest man out of me.'

At dinner it became apparent that his parents weren't sitting in judgement on Luis; they were worried about how he saw them. They feared being perceived as bad parents and were trying to impress upon Luis that the estrangement had never been about a lack of love. To this end they arrived with evidence: photos of Danny as a happy child – including one he had never seen before, on the beach at Bude with his dad holding him in the air, joyful in a way that only children can be. His father said, 'He was the happiest child.'

This description had always needled Danny, sounding to his ear like a lament, implying that he was a boy who had lost his happiness when he realized he was gay. His parents hadn't fucked him up, being gay had. But watching his parents share the stories behind these photos Danny understood that these were the years when they were most proud of their parenting.

After the main course Luis brought out a tray of Spanish desserts, a slab of hazelnut-studded nougat, sweet-filled pastries and the almond cake that Danny had baked for the occasion served warm with vanilla ice cream. His mother seized on a lull in the conversation to make an announcement, opening her bag and offering Luis a smartly printed leaflet about the guest house.

'If you do decide to move to Spain, to make a life there, we'd love to host your wedding at our guest house.'

His father elaborated. 'Luis, we appreciate you haven't seen our place, which we feel bad about. To make amends we'll set aside that weekend. The whole house would be for you and your guests. It would be our gift. We know you can't say yes or no right now but we wanted the two of you to be aware of the option if it all works out. Which we hope it does. I told Danny at Christmas that the two of you have made a beautiful home here. I have no doubt you can do the same in Spain.'

Danny placed a finger on the photo of him on the beach in Bude being held aloft by his dad.

'I don't know if I can ever feel this happy again. But right now, I'm close.'

Luis reached over and took Danny's hand. A revolutionary gesture.

# Chapter Thirty-Nine

## *The Story Luis Never Told*

Danny and Luis arrived in Spain on Saturday, 22 March, the Iberia flight touching down at midday in the southern city of Sevilla. A light rain shower cleared by the time they reached their small hotel, a converted mansion once belonging to nineteenth-century spice traders. The façade was white, gleaming after the rain, with wrought-iron bars on the lower floor windows and wooden shutters on the upper floors. Wide-eyed at the beauty of this city, Danny reminded himself that he was not travelling as a tourist – he was asking whether this country could be home. Who he would be here, who Luis would be – who they might be together.

In the weeks before the departure Luis and Danny attended couples therapy for the first time in their relationship. They were recommended a Soho-based practice, a collective of counsellors whose private clients funded their charity work with teenagers kicked out of their homes for being gay. They requested sessions with the most experienced counsellor, a man born in Amman, Jordan, who moved to England to study psychology at University College London. He had written an acclaimed book about reconciling sexuality with faith. Luis read the book in a single Sunday before their first session. Seated side by side in a small room with a box of tissues between them Luis and Danny talked about the events of their engagement, their separation, and their lives preceding it. Danny described the absence of any physical intimacy in public and Luis described his dependency upon professional success. After both Danny and Luis depicted their relationship as being like a lifeboat in the early years, seeking refuge from the world, the therapist mentioned the Ship of Theseus paradox, a thought experiment. If, over time, a boat's timbers are replaced one by one, does it remain the same boat? The parallel was clear: over time, their relationship had maintained the same shape yet the timbers of these two men had changed. The marriage proposal had been a way of asking them to abandon the lifeboat analogy and accept they were no longer in stormy oceans. Perhaps it was time for a sailboat – swift, elegant and visible.

Entering their hotel room Danny found a welcome card addressing them as 'Mr & Mr'. It was presented beside a selection of miniature pastries under a glass cloche with an accompanying bottle of Oloroso sherry from the nearby town of Jerez. Helping himself to a *pestiño*, an Easter delicacy, Danny stepped onto their small stone terrace to admire the vista of church towers, washing lines, television aerials and red roof tiles. When Luis joined him, Danny remarked, 'You made a fuss.'

After having sex in the shower – 'I can feel your heartbeat inside me,' Danny had said – they left the hotel and strolled through Santa Cruz, the old Jewish Quarter where the streets were so narrow some houses on opposite sides were barely an arm's length apart. They allowed themselves to become lost, turning right and left without checking their map, arriving at a high-walled botanical garden. The blossoms and buds were bright after the morning's rain. The scent was strong. Like curious children they placed their hands on the massive trunks of two-hundred-year-old Moreton Bay fig trees which resembled dinosaur legs, their buttress roots splayed across the soil.

At the river Danny and Luis stopped at a café, enjoying a glass of dark vermouth served with a wedge of fresh orange. Luis described how Sevilla had always been a place of wonder to him. Light-headed from the alcohol and the excitement of their visit, Danny asked, 'How did you ever leave this place behind?'

Luis looked at Danny, weighing whether to answer that question completely. This was why they had come to

Spain – to tell truths. Speaking in a voice so soft it was as if he were talking to himself, he said, 'After I left home, I fled to Madrid, and like you, stayed with friends, sleeping on sofas. I behaved as I'd never behaved before. Recklessly. Bars and clubs. Everything I had denied myself I allowed myself. That summer I met a man. He was somewhere between a friend and a boyfriend. We hung out. We slept together. One day he asked if I wanted to smoke heroin together. And I said okay.'

In all their years Luis had never even smoked pot. He had been emphatic from the beginning that he didn't do drugs of any kind. Noticing Danny's reaction Luis elaborated. 'Heroin wasn't as unthinkable as it sounds. There were no needles or spoons. We'd melt it on a sheet of tin foil and inhale the smoke with a rolled-up note.'

'What was it like?'

'It was like my troubles were made of ice. When I smoked, the ice cubes melted away – like I'd thrown them out into the midday sun. In a few minutes, I felt good in a way I thought was lost to me. I remember sitting on a patch of dry yellow grass outside a block of apartments in La Latina district, like a stray dog, yet I felt like a king. The whole world seemed to be a beautiful movie, the dead grass, the cracked paint, the blue sky. I was watching my life from the back row of an auditorium in the world's most comfortable seat.'

The waiter returned asking if they wanted more vermouth and Danny, using his limited Spanish, made the effort to order two more. Neither of them spoke until the fresh glasses were returned.

Luis continued, 'We would go to the Parque de Atracciones, the amusement park in Madrid, doped up, sitting in the front carriage of a rollercoaster. We didn't make a sound while everyone behind us was screaming with their arms in the air. By the end of August, the heat was unbearable, so we caught a train to Valencia, where he had a friend, to hang out on the beach. The beach there is big, not pretty like the Costa Brava – more a motorway of sand. We smoked and sat under the shadow of a bent parasol we found discarded in a bin. I remember the sea was shallow and the water was warm. One day I waded out into the sea, holding my shorts up – I'd lost so much weight. The water was lapping at my knees. To my right there were the port's industrial cranes. And I wondered about all the boats unloading their cargo. Where had they come from? What were they carrying? The kind of questions kids ask. When I turned towards the beach there was a lifeguard. I thought to myself – that man used to be me. It had been my summer job. And it dawned on me. I wasn't making my life easier. I was making my life smaller. I pictured it as a circle. It had shrunk to the size of a speck – waking up, smoking, scoring, swimming, smoking, fucking, sleeping. When I returned to the beach I sat down on our dirty towel, under our bent parasol, and I said to my friend – let's quit, today, right now, while we can. While we're young and healthy. Let's live again. He said no. I saw in his eyes he was afraid. I begged him, as I had begged Isabella, only I couldn't cry anymore. He said he would find me after the summer. Of course, he never did.'

Luis took a sip of his vermouth.

'When I returned to Spain this winter, I discovered that he had died many years ago. I should have dragged him from that beach, but I didn't. I left him there, went back to Madrid and never touched drugs again. When I arrived in London, work was my addiction. I worked harder than I had ever worked before. Even with success there was a numbness inside of me. Until I met you. I had gone to that bar for a hook-up. Yet once we were together, I didn't want you to leave. I was so worried you might find me needy, holding you tight in bed. You might see what a broken man I was. And how many broken people I had left in my wake. That's why I never spoke about the past. Not because it was better. I almost didn't survive it.'

# Chapter Forty

## *Communion*

Following a breakfast of fresh pastries and black coffee, Luis and Danny visited La Catedral de Santa María de la Sede. Inside Luis took a seat near the front facing the gilded altarpiece in the area designated for private prayer. Danny lingered in the aisle until Luis gestured for him to join him. Speaking in a hushed confessional tone Luis spoke about his first communion in Cádiz.

'My priest was Father Rafael López. He could speak intelligently on almost any subject. He read eighty books a year. He advised me, educated me – adopted me, in a way. When I wanted to hide from my parents, I hid with him. For many years I imagined my future was to become a priest, an ambition he encouraged until I was engaged. When he discovered that I was gay, he never spoke to me again, as if a shop's shutters had been pulled down. He would walk past me on the street, I would say his name and he wouldn't turn around. At the time many people were reacting this way, so I thought his disgust was the same. Years later I reconsidered his actions. It occurred to me that he might have been gay as well. With the scandals in the Catholic Church, he must have been terrified that people would presume he was involved with me sexually. I made him guilty by association. I wonder if he had always known the truth about me – that I was a man like him, which was why he was guiding me towards priesthood, celibacy being the only path he could offer. This winter I traced him. Father Lopez left Cádiz not long after I left and transferred to a church in Argentina where he lived out his life. I made exiles of both of us.'

Luis turned towards the altar as if this were now a silent conversation between him and his church.

As they left the nave and walked out into a courtyard of trimmed citrus trees Danny admitted, 'I've always felt ashamed of how little I knew about your past, your family, your faith, but maybe that was part of my appeal? That I was so far from this world, this place, your people, that I never reminded you of everything you had lost? In the same way London was an escape, I was an escape.'

Luis accepted the point.

'It might have been part of it.'

Danny asked, 'If that was the attraction of me *then*, what draws you to me *now* when there's nothing to hide?'

Luis looked up at the orange tree and placed his hand on one of the still-green fruits.

'I don't want to marry the man who doesn't know me. I want to marry the man who knows me.'

On Sunday night they attended the Semana Santa procession, a parade of ornate *pasos* depicting scenes from the Passion of Christ, with pedestals painted in gold leaf and hemmed with velvet. The floats were carried by *costaleros* chosen from the community who considered the task to be a great honour. Luis explained that he had left for England before he could have been chosen. Many were illuminated by candles, some wax and wick, others electric. According to Luis a few of the same floats were involved in the parades he attended as a child, maintained and restored over the years he had been away. As the *pasos* filed by, Luis recognized them individually, like they were old school friends, and he appeared quite overwhelmed.

The next day they caught a train to the coastal town of Cádiz with the intention of meeting Luis's mother for dinner. As they neared the final stop the train passed through salt flats and flocks of flamingos. An observation occurred to Danny – they were two kids from the coast, lovers of the sea, forced to leave it behind. Since their luggage was light, they opted to walk from Cádiz station rather than wait for a taxi, arriving at the Parador Hotel. It was situated on the tip of the peninsula, a modern building with floor-to-ceiling glass windows and sea views from every terrace.

Keen to enjoy the remains of the day, they checked in and left the hotel, walking along the promenade to the adjacent beach, a sheltered cove dotted with old timber fishing boats and flanked on either side by the *castillos* of Santa Catalina and San Sebastián. It was the beach where Luis had proposed to Isabella. In Danny's imagination the location was flawlessly romantic. The beach was certainly attractive but no more romantic than the Scottish Highlands, a practical choice for a young man living in town, escaping the bustle of the bars, in search of a secluded place. Danny crouched down, squeezing a handful of the sand as if searching for some imprint of the memory.

Luis touched his shoulder and pointed to the sea. They crossed an outcrop of jagged rocks that began at the base of the castle fortifications and extended into the water. The tide was low, exposing a plateau of barnacled stone. There were old men in thick knitwear. By their rubber boots were plastic buckets filled with crabs. Many of the men were teamed with their grandchildren who delighted in each catch. Walking in a zigzag to avoid the deep crevices, Danny and Luis reached the furthest edge of the plateau. Luis explained that he'd often stood here as a child. Danny was reminded of how he would swim out to sea off the coast of Bude, looking back at his hometown as if it were something other to him or as if he were something other to it, and he wondered if Luis had been doing something similar. In the distance one of the older crab-collecting men waved at them, bellowing words into the wind. Luis translated, 'We're about to be caught by the tide.'

Incoming waves broke over their shoes.

Walking back to the hotel, with damp shoes and damp socks, Luis asked a passer-by to take their photo as a couple, something they had never asked a stranger to do before. They stood with the beach behind them, their arms around each other. When the phone was handed back the woman said they made a handsome couple. To anyone watching it was the most ordinary of events. But Danny and Luis studied the photo as though it were a magnificent seashell they had found on the sand.

With only a few hours before dinner they decided to delay exploring the old town until the following day. Luis wanted to rest beforehand. While he slept, fully clothed atop the duvet, Danny sat on the terrace, practising simple Spanish phrases as the sky darkened. After sunset he showered and shaved before ironing his black cotton trousers and a white shirt. He noticed his hands were shaking.

*

Luis's mother lived on Alameda Hermanas Carvia Bernal, a street on the edge of the old town in a former customs house dating back two hundred years, converted to apartments at the turn of the twentieth century. The front-facing apartments offered occupants unimpeded sea views over the coastal defences. These were not modest family homes. Luis had been born into wealth. He said, 'My father was always after my mother's money. Her parents warned her about him. But she ignored them, believing they were in love. She saw herself as courageous, breaking the convention of marrying within her social class. After the marriage her parents provided this apartment where we were allowed to live but never allowed to sell. On some level my mother saw my being gay as a repeat of her folly in love. Conventions exist for a reason. You should never follow your heart.'

After Luis spoke into the intercom, the front door was buzzed open and they entered an elegant hallway lined with patterned ceramic tiles. In the central stairway there was a birdcage elevator encased in ornate iron. Rather than use it, they climbed the stone stairs to the second floor, knocking on the double doors. Only now did it occur to Danny that they hadn't brought any gifts.

'I can't meet your mother empty-handed. I'll be back. There was a shop nearby.'

Before Luis could disagree, Danny ran down the stairs and out of the main door.

In a nearby minimarket Danny bought the most expensive bottle of red wine he could find and, unable to see any flowers, a selection of marzipan truffles that rattled around in a decorative tin. He returned to the apartment, steadying himself before ringing the intercom, forced to make use of his limited Spanish. In the hotel room he had checked over this vocabulary a hundred times. But to his ear he sounded ridiculous. Luis's mother buzzed him in.

# Chapter Forty-One

## *A Table by the Window*

Luis's eyes were the same green colour as his mother's. At the age of seventy-two, she dressed formally, like an Andalusian aristocrat from another era. Her silver hair was put up with an Art Nouveau pin designed as a cluster of irises with faded blue petals. She wore a white silk shirt, pleated trousers and black sandals. Though she was an imposing figure, Danny's instinct was to feel great affection for her if for no more complicated a reason than she was the mother of the man he loved. With a slight bow Danny handed her the bottle of wine and marzipan chocolates, which appeared absurd in her elegant hands. Luis's hands were behind his back. He seemed to have regressed to the role of a well-behaved boy who knew his place. His mother's name was Cristina and although she spoke a few words of crisp English, she preferred to speak Spanish. Trying to win her over Danny pointed at the hairpin and told her how much he liked it. She thanked him, overlooking his accent, before gesturing for them to follow her. They passed through a once-grand dining room with wood-panelled walls. A crystal chandelier was wrapped in protective sheets. There were marks on the floor and shadows on the walls where furniture had once stood, and art once hung. Only in the kitchen did the apartment come alive, filled with potted plants, books, newspapers and ashtrays. It appeared as if Cristina had retreated inside her own home, abandoning entire rooms until her existence revolved around a small table by the window with a view of the sea.

The table was attractively laid with a lace tablecloth, embroidered cotton napkins, hand-painted ceramic plates, heavy silver cutlery and stemless *chato* glasses for wine. In the middle stood a majolica vase filled with delicate white poppies and a wicker basket of unevenly sliced *pan manolete*. For dinner Cristina had prepared two stews. There was a vegetarian *tagarninas* stew made from oyster thistle with wild garlic, in addition to an *arroz negro* with cuttlefish. Luis carried the cast-iron dishes from the oven and the three of them sat so close their knees brushed against each other. Danny helped himself to both dishes. They were delicious, he said. Luis led the conversation, translating only at natural breaks.

As they neared the end of the meal Cristina reached out

towards Danny and Luis explained, 'My mother would like to hold your hands.'

Putting down his knife and fork Danny gladly gave his hands to her, wondering if there was a spiritual dimension to the request. The opposite seemed to be true; she held his hands as though trying to understand him as a physical reality. Danny had never cared for his hands which were calloused from hospital work with his nails clipped short for reasons of hygiene. Luis spoke to his mother for a time, while she continued to hold Danny's hands, and he could feel her reactions to the exchange. She let go, returning her hands to her legs. Luis took a sip of wine before translating.

'I invited my mother to our wedding. She can't come. She thanks us for the invitation but said she is too old to leave Cádiz.'

Luis had opened his heart and was now processing the rejection he had feared.

They ate in silence for a time until, with a sharper tone, Luis turned back to his mother. Danny couldn't follow the meaning but even without understanding the vocabulary the hurt was unmistakable. A few times he caught the Spanish word for father. In previous conversations Luis had described cutting off contact with his dad many years ago. This winter he had discovered that his father had long since moved out of the town, divorcing Cristina and marrying another woman. Luis had made it clear to Danny that even if his father sought a reconciliation and wanted to come to the wedding, he would not be welcome. He would find a way to undermine the ceremony, to ridicule and belittle it. He was a destructive force. Sounding upset, Luis summarized the conversation for Danny.

'My father is in a nursing home in Motril near Granada. When my mother visits, he pretends not to remember her because he is too proud to acknowledge her kindness which he does not deserve.'

Danny asked, 'What were you disagreeing about?'

Ever the lawyer, Luis pointed out the inconsistency in his mother's reasoning.

'She turned down our wedding invitation because she said she is too old to leave Cádiz. But she does leave, once a month, to visit my father, a man who pretends not to know who she is, a man who stole from her, cheated on her, hit her. Yet she still dotes upon him. She will travel to be by his side, but she won't come to our wedding.'

Danny observed, 'Granada isn't far, though?'

Luis refused to accept this excuse.

'She doesn't own a car. She takes the train to Sevilla, catches a bus to Granada and another bus to Motril. It probably takes six hours, all to visit a man who won't say her name.'

Abruptly Luis stood up to leave. Cristina remained seated, looking up. For a moment Danny imagined her standing up, wrapping her arms around her son to stop him from running away again. Perhaps she imagined it too. Luis left the table without another word. Unsure what to do Danny remained seated. Cristina lit a cigarette and indicated that Danny should follow. He nodded, standing up and walking to the doorway where he stopped, turning back to Cristina. Impulsively, Danny fetched an ashtray from the windowsill and placed it on the table for her. Glancing up at him, she noticed the silver crucifix around his neck. She recognized it, reached out and touched it. It had once belonged to her father.

Outside Danny hurried to catch up with Luis, who was already some distance away. Reaching his side, as they passed through the gates of Parque Genovés, Danny touched his arm. Luis didn't slow down.

'Your mother will come to our wedding.'

Luis shook his head as if Danny simply hadn't understood the conversation.

'Luis, listen to me. She wore irises in her hair. And she dressed up for dinner. She made us two stews. She laid the table with silver cutlery and embroidered napkins. She filled a vase with poppies. And she held my hand. The way she held it, it felt kind and curious. She's nervous about coming to England. Nervous that everyone at the wedding will judge her. The same way my parents were scared when they met you. As for your father, maybe she visits him because even though he was a bad husband, she's a good wife. She's a romantic, like you. She swore a vow to him no matter how badly he behaved.'

Luis stopped walking.

'You like her?'

Danny nodded.

'Very much.'

'We were inseparable, once.'

Danny replied, 'I can tell.'

'I miss her.'

'She misses you too.'

Weighing whether to go back, Luis sat on a park bench. Danny joined him, placing an arm across his back. The pair of them waited while a young couple on their first date wandered through the tropical plants and ancient trees hoping for a kiss.

# Chapter Forty-Two

## *A Portrait of Luis*

The next morning Danny and Luis woke early to watch the sunrise. After showering, Luis picked out a pair of linen trousers the colour of clay and a cotton shirt. There was a monastic simplicity to his clothes. Among the first to arrive at the hotel's buffet breakfast, they helped themselves to glasses of pulpy orange juice and plates of sliced fruit. Acting on a whim Danny layered a slice of toast with hazelnut-chocolate spread, cream cheese and peach jam, laughing like a kid on holiday as he took a messy bite, not the least bit worried about the meeting with Isabella, the woman Luis had once been engaged to.

Located near the historic centre, Isabella's gallery was nestled between a florist and a tobacco store with clay pots of red geraniums on one side and an array of handmade briar pipes on the other. Outside the front window there was a low backless bench where an older man happened to be resting in the morning sun, shopping bags filled with loose vegetables by his side. Danny and Luis said good morning to him as they entered the gallery where Isabella was waiting. They found her in a small office that looked out onto a plant-filled courtyard. She was brewing coffee and when she saw them, she paused and looked them up and down. She was slim with glossy auburn hair. Her eyes were bright blue. Luis mentioned that she loved to sail and it was easy to imagine her moving across the bow of a ship, tying ropes and securing sails. She and Luis hugged with cautious intimacy while Danny stood a few steps back, observing their interaction. Despite their complex history it seemed apparent that whatever heartache she'd once experienced, these wounds healed a long time ago. For Luis, it wasn't so clear.

Isabella and Danny politely shook hands and he did his best with the Spanish greetings he had memorized. She made no attempt to hide her scrutiny. While serving three aromatic black coffees, the smell mingling with a back note of turpentine from the nearby studio, Isabella offered a tour. The paintings for sale were by a collective of local artists who co-owned the gallery. There were depictions of the city and the coastline including fishing boats, churches and town squares. Isabella's paintings were the most unusual of the collection. She painted the salt flats on the outskirts.

Danny admired them, sincere in his praise, growing less embarrassed by his efforts at Spanish. Luis seemed cooler in his response, saying little. Over breakfast he had mentioned her fascination with people's bodies as they worked, the shapes they formed, in a shop or on the street. She caught Luis's look and said, 'It's hard to make a living from painting people. No one wants to buy a painting of a stranger's face. Mostly we sell to tourists, who want a memory of the city, or hotel owners who want a painting for their lobby.'

At the end of the tour Luis and Isabella caught up in the courtyard. Danny had offered to leave them alone but they insisted on him staying with them. The sound of their conversation in Spanish was comforting even if Danny was unable to follow most of it. He wondered why she had chosen the gallery as a venue for their meeting, uncertain about bringing Luis into her home with her two sons and husband, concerned that she would be presenting the life he could have lived. Luis had discussed the idea of inviting her to the wedding. Danny was supportive, particularly after he heard that Isabella had reached out many years ago and invited Luis to her wedding, an offer he had declined, and a fact Luis had never shared with him at the time. This was why he had proposed, Danny thought, to reveal all these unseen textures and incidents that he had sensed but never understood. Switching into English, Luis drew Danny into the conversation.

'The hope is that we might marry this summer. If we do, we would like to invite you and your family to the wedding.'

Isabella congratulated them. But she seemed awkward at the invitation to the ceremony. Speaking in English she explained that it was difficult to travel with the children because of her work commitments. Danny interjected, to make his feelings clear.

'We'd love for you to be there.'

Isabella looked at Danny, perceiving the deeper significance of the invitation.

'I will try.'

She promised to talk to Luis's mother about the arrangements and perhaps they could travel together.

Luis asked, 'How do you know my mother wants to come?'

Isabella seemed surprised.

'Of course she will come.'

And it was true. Last night, after Danny and Luis returned to the apartment, Cristina had served them dessert and changed her mind. She apologized for saying 'no' and promised to attend.

Isabella gestured for them to wait in the courtyard while she went into the gallery, returning a few minutes later with a painting carefully wrapped in unbleached canvas. It was a portrait she'd painted of Luis over thirty years ago. It depicted him as a handsome young man, bare-chested, his shoulders thrown back. The setting was a rural barn. He was holding a rooster. The sunset was lava red, as if the sky were on fire. His gaze was not directed at the artist but towards arid fields of ploughed earth. To Danny it was an honest rendering of the man he loved, capturing his strength along with his mystery. With deft ambiguity, it was hard to tell if Luis was caring for the rooster or about to slaughter it. Danny guessed from the painting that she knew the truth about Luis before being told. She handed the portrait to Danny as if entrusting him with a part of Luis's heart.

# Chapter Forty-Three

## *Where Now?*

Nearing the end of their stay in Spain Luis rented a car, planning a trip to a mystery destination he claimed was inaccessible by public transport, refusing to say where they were going or why. Danny guessed that the location was connected to the many discussions Luis had enjoyed with his mother over recent days, sometimes the two of them on their own, mostly the three of them together, including a sunny afternoon on the beach where Luis had once worked as a lifeguard. Since it was warm Danny had suggested that they swim. Although Luis pointed out that many of the town residents were still wearing jackets and jumpers he eventually acquiesced. They stripped to their underwear, the only bathers on the long eastern stretch of Playa de la Victoria, while Cristina perched on a lounger sheltering under a raffia hat. With the entire sea to themselves Luis and Danny splashed about with childish joyful abandon, an impressive feat considering they were both nearing fifty. In his hometown, in front of his mother, Luis lifted Danny into the air before they tumbled into the water.

They warmed up with *carajillos* – coffee fortified with a shot of brandy at a beachside café. Inspired by the sight of their physical interaction Cristina spoke openly about why she had married Luis's father. She had believed it was possible to judge a man from the passion of their physical intimacy. And based on their kisses she had been sure that they were soulmates. She had spent a lifetime waiting for him to live up to the promise of their sexual connection. In love there were two types of tragedy: the good man with a bad kiss and the bad man with a good kiss. She was pleased Luis had found a kind man who kissed well. Hearing the translation, Danny blushed.

On the last weekend before returning to London Danny and Luis collected the rental car, a silver Volkswagen convertible, perfect for a road trip. Since it was another warm day Luis lowered the car's roof. Driving out of the city felt like embarking on the adventure Danny imagined their marriage would be. Before departing Cádiz they stopped at a bakery to buy two paper-wrapped *barras de pan*, one filled with *jamón*, another with *queso de cabra*, along with two bottles of sparkling mineral water from the mountain springs in

Catalonia. Enigmatically Luis claimed there were no shops where they were going.

The scenic drive took over two hours, passing through Parque Natural de Los Alcornocales before arriving at the small historic hillside town of Jimena de la Frontera. Though the town was pretty, Luis didn't stop, following a road further up the hill. At this point he slowed to a crawl until he found a turn-off. They bumped along a narrow dirt track for a time, reaching a rusted metal gate where Luis parked. Danny stepped out and surveyed the area. Though they were high in the hills there was no panoramic view as they were surrounded by a plantation of tall oaks. Luis explained that these trees were harvested for their bark which was turned into corks for the region's wine. Many of the trunks were banded where the cork had been stripped back. To the chatter of birds Luis led the way, lifting the latch on the rusted gate.

Danny asked, 'Isn't this private property?'

Luis nodded.

'My grandparents owned this farm.'

Since his grandparents had died many years ago, Danny wondered, 'Who lives here now?'

Luis replied, 'We could.'

# Chapter Forty-Four

## *A Different Kind of Life*

The oak plantation thinned as they climbed the steep dirt track, reaching an elevated plateau beneath a sheer ridge, sheltered from the prevailing winds and shaded from the afternoon sun. The word Luis used to describe the farm was *cortijo*, and it comprised three stone houses arranged with the largest in the middle and the two smaller ones either side. Between the houses were almond trees and in the walled remains of a fire pit, charcoal dust was speckled with wildflowers. At the perimeter were taller orange and lemon trees with unkempt branches and a legacy of rotten fruit underneath. Like impacted teeth, sandstone boulders jutted out of the soil. Some of the smaller rocks served as a place for chopping firewood, evidenced by chinks in the stone, while others were smoothed from mounting horses. Seed pods drifted through the air, seeming to slow to take in the beauty of this place, a forgotten world. Standing in the dappled sunlight with his hands on his waist, Luis took on the appearance of a renowned explorer who had rediscovered the lost city he had been searching for his entire life – the lost city of home.

Scattered around the three houses were the ruins of stables and barns with sloping roofs and faded tiles. A herd of free-roaming goats had followed them up the hill and began grazing among the buildings, their bells overpowering the birdsong. Despite the dilapidated condition of the farm only a modest act of imagination was required to picture its past, not one of subsistence or rural drudgery but of abundance. The walls of the main buildings were decorated with blue ceramic *azulejo* panels of the Virgin Mary. Beside them wrought–iron lanterns of exceptional craftsmanship hung outside massive timber doors. The doors were engraved with fantastical images, including dragons, castles and knights. The main house was unlocked but the hinges were stiff with age and it required the strength of them both to push the door open.

Inside Danny and Luis stood on a stone slab floor. Much of the original furniture remained, an oak table and hand-carved chairs. There was a clay oven patiently waiting for life to return. The air inside the house was cooler. The layout had been cleverly designed, a breeze flowing through the horseshoe–shaped open doorways. At the back there were two small bedrooms on either side of the hall. In one there was a porcelain crucifix on the wall and when Danny looked closer, a pale pink gecko sheltered behind it, with fragile translucent skin.

Climbing the uneven stone stairs to the roof Danny and Luis emerged onto the terrace which offered a view through the break in the treeline. The terrace was crowded with urns, some made of clay and prettily painted, others mottled and without decoration. During the long hot summers when the *cortijo* stood abandoned most of the potted plants had died, reduced to wilted stalks except for the largest urn where a hardy Ginkgo biloba tree had survived, cascading its roots over the edge, finding soil in the surrounding urns, scavenging water from drops of morning dew.

Looking out over the land Luis said, 'My grandparents hoped that one day I would take over this farm. My father would've sold the land for a barrel of wine, so their only hope was me. They taught me many of the skills needed to live here from horsemanship to carpentry.'

Danny asked, 'Is this home for you?'

Luis held on to the question for a time before asking one of his own.

'Could it be home for you?'

Danny sat on the wall, staring at the olive trees.

'It would be unlike any life I've ever known.'

Luis agreed.

Danny continued, 'It would be unlike any life I ever felt suited for.'

Luis reacted to the limitation Danny placed on himself.

'We always believed big cities were our friends because they let us be anonymous there. We don't need to be anonymous anymore. And if we live here, everyone will know us.'

'As what? The two fags in a farm on a hill?'

Luis didn't miss a beat.

'Some might say that. A few. So be it. Danny, you dreamed of a garden.'

Danny laughed, 'Luis, this is more than a garden.'

Luis sat beside Danny.

'It's a way of life. This place was always more than a farm. My grandparents allowed friends with no money to stay. The outhouses were filled with people down on their luck – poets, artists and musicians. They would compose songs and paint in exchange for a few hours' work in the fields. Before I left Cádiz in disgrace, I visited my grandfather here. He could barely look me in the eye. But he prophesized that one day I would return. At the time I thought he meant that being gay was a fad, an act of madness that would pass. Today, I believe he meant that nothing had changed in his heart about me. He didn't know how to say it. And I didn't know how to hear it.'

Danny's fingers explored the leaves of the ginkgo tree.

'Describe an ordinary day.'

Luis inhaled the air of his ancestor's farm.

'We would wake with the sun, breakfast on the roof or

on the terrace. Afterwards, we might harvest the almonds to make butter which we can spread on the bread you would bake in our oven. We would press our olives, which we can use to roast the vegetables we grow on the slopes. We would still work, as we saw fit. Me as a lawyer. In the small towns. You as a nurse. We would invite our friends and family to stay with us when they needed to escape. Your parents. My mother. All these buildings will be repaired and restored and full of people we love. In the evenings we would sit around the fire and listen to their stories.'

Though captivated by the vision, Danny noted, 'I will always be an outsider here.'

Luis shook his head.

'Up here, there are no outsiders.'

Standing up on the ledge, excited by the scale of the change, Danny pointed out, 'Luis, we don't even own the land.'

But Luis was ready for the question.

'The farm is held in a family trust. If I restore it and live here, the title passes to me and my spouse. My grandfather was a cautious man. Only after a meaningful amount of time living here would it become ours.'

Danny picked at the words.

'How long is a meaningful amount of time?'

A faint smile appeared across Luis's lips.

'Twenty years.'

Your presence is requested at

## The Marriage

of

## Luis Lagana & Daniel Smith

On

## 20th July 2013

At Three in the Afternoon

Dinner and Dancing to Follow

Please Note the Change of Venue
Bude Guest House
Cornwall
England

# Chapter Forty-Five

## *The Marriage Act*

Danny couldn't believe it. Three days before the wedding Parliament passed a gay marriage law. He had completed his last shift at St Thomas' Hospital, packed up the apartment and should have been getting ready to travel to Bude but all he could do was watch the news – preoccupied with the coverage as the Marriage (Same Sex Couples) Act 2013 received Royal Assent. The same-sex part had been tucked away in a gut-punch of a parenthesis, implying the institution of marriage was the important part and if a few gays wanted to pay homage to the institution, so be it. Pacing in front of the television, heckling the pundits like a football fan, Danny watched as broadcasters reported the public polls – fifty-five per cent for, forty-five per cent against, described as a 'slim majority' and requiring 'great courage' from politicians.

Despite fierce opposition England and Wales became the sixteenth countries in the world to legalize gay marriage. As Danny scrambled to figure out if they would be able to call their upcoming wedding a wedding and their marriage a marriage, he realized the implementation of the law would be too late for their ceremony. Gay weddings would not be permitted until the following spring. Digital 'Save the Date' fliers released by campaigners popped across the internet – 'First Gay Marriages: 29 March 2014'. Almost a year away. Danny and Luis's civil ceremony would be caught in the legislative gap – out-of-date the moment they said their vows.

That night Danny and Luis watched the ten o'clock news seated on the floor of their recently sold apartment, their home for so many years, now standing almost empty. A few sentimental pieces had been shipped to Spain, Luis's beloved reading chair, his antique lamp, their books, but much had been sold or given away, not suited to a farm on an Andalusian hill. Luis and Danny intended to redecorate when they arrived, slowly, over many months – gradually finding furniture and crockery from markets and artisans in the area. Starting anew. Before the bulletin had even finished, wedding guests began ringing Danny and Luis to congratulate them, convinced that the passing of the Bill meant they would be attending one of the first gay marriages in the country. How amazing, they said, to be part of history. Some hoped there might be television cameras to capture the event, disappointed to discover they would be among some of the final guests attending a 'civil partnership ceremony', the antiquated term as dry as a mouthful of crackers. Danny consoled them that they planned to convert the civil partnership to marriage as soon as they arrived in Spain. Funny, really, because critics of the law had called gay marriage a 'phoney currency', and here they were converting it at the border, in a country where gay marriages had been legal tender for eight years. Asked why they chose to marry in England, rather than Spain, Danny replied that they had found the perfect venue in England. And they weren't about to change their plans based on the whims of a government. Whatever the paperwork called it, they would call it a wedding. Luis and Danny were getting married on Saturday, the law could catch up.

# Chapter Forty-Six

## *Stitching*

On the night before the wedding Luis and Danny were in the attic suite of the Bude Guest House inspecting their wedding suits which had been tailored in Cádiz. The tailors were an elderly husband-and-wife team who had designed Cristina's clothes for over forty years and, when asked if they would make suits for a gay marriage, simply said, '*Y por qué no?*'

Since Luis and Danny had missed the Savile Row deadline they had their measurements taken in Cádiz instead. Luis had suggested that the suits be made from linen woven in Cambrai using northern French flax famed for its softness. One of the suits was lavender while the other was juniper-green – the colours of the flax plant and flower from which they were made. On the green suit the stitching was lavender. On the lavender suit the stitching was green. They would wear them with white cotton shirts. No ties, no belts – nothing to cinch, nothing to hide. Luis would wear the lavender. Danny would wear the green.

Cristina and Isabella had brought the finished suits with them to England. They were not the only Spanish guests. News of the wedding had spread. Four of Luis's school friends asked if they could attend along with their wives. Soon more than twenty people were coming from Madrid, Sevilla and Cádiz. The invitation list swelled to over one hundred and forty as many people in Bude also wanted to take part in the celebrations, some who knew Danny as a child, others who knew him from the descriptions in his parents' Christmas cards, everyone wanting to feel part of this new era, creating the mood of a small-town fête.

Jasper had driven down from London early in the morning. He was in excellent spirits, pleased with the arrangements and delighted to share the work with Danny's parents. Preparations had progressed so smoothly they were already brainstorming future collaborations. Jasper thought that the guest house was a magical setting for a wedding. Studying the suits, he nodded.

'They're a pair.'

Before adding, 'We don't have to follow every convention. But some are worth following.'

Luis and Danny agreed not to see each other dressed in

their suits until the wedding itself. Luis indicated that Danny should try his suit on first, stepping out of the bedroom and taking Isabella with him. Cristina, herself an excellent seamstress, remained behind with Jasper ready to make any alterations. Danny entered the bathroom, the room he regularly cleaned as a lonely teenager, now the changing room for his wedding. The suit was a perfect fit. He paused, resting on the sink, anxious about feeling so happy – reminding himself happiness was real, the anxiety was fleeting, not the other way round. He opened the door and gave his appreciative audience a twirl.

Abiding by another convention, Danny planned to spend the night apart from Luis, sleeping in his old bedroom at his parents' house while Luis stayed in the guest house. That night Danny and his parents sat in the back garden sharing a pot of herbal tea. In advance of the wedding, Danny had quit drinking and vaping. He couldn't exactly say why, only that he'd outgrown both. The three of them spoke late into the night. Danny's mother and father told stories about their own wedding, most of which he had never heard before. A bungled speech. The public joy and secret sadness of Danny's grandfather, the last wedding he attended before he died. After they said goodnight to each other Danny lay in bed, savouring the anticipation. At around three in the morning, exhaustion overtook him, and he nodded off.

*

At sunrise, Danny's first thought was that today was the day he was going to be married. In the kitchen his mother and father prepared a shared breakfast platter of buttery scrambled eggs from the local farm and roasted tomatoes from their garden. Danny ate a hearty portion.

Serving him with a pot of strong tea his mother asked, 'How are you feeling?'

He replied, 'I feel ready.'

The forecast was overcast, with the risk of midday rain clearing in time for the afternoon ceremony. Jasper had organized a bad-weather plan but Danny was irrationally certain that the rain would pass and the sun would shine. Jasper arrived after breakfast dressed in his red wedding attire, his double-breasted jacket and red tie with a blue cornflower affixed to his lapel. He checked his meticulous notes.

'Guest-wise, there are a few delays with the trains. It still looks like everyone is going to make it in time. On the weather front we're holding back setting up the terrace until after the rain has cleared. As for your schedule, it's very light. You're going to change here with some help from your friends. Individual photos in the garden with your parents while I'm working on the terrace.'

Danny asked, 'How's Luis?'

Jasper glanced at him.

'When I left the guest house he twas having breakfast with his family and friends. He seems relaxed.'

As Jasper was leaving, Matt and Sophie arrived, already dressed for the ceremony. Sophie was wearing a pair of pleated trousers with an oblique-front jacket fastened with a single button. Bold and brilliant. Matt was wearing navy blue trousers with loafers, a white shirt and a skinny pink tie. They had met at the welcome drinks last night and were already friends. Still in his tracksuit, Danny sat on the edge of his single bed while his two friends fussed over his face using cleanser and toner. It was funny, intimate, and it gave them something to do. As forecast, a rain shower passed over the area and the three of them paused to watch. Within thirty minutes the rain cleared, leaving broken cloud and patches of soft blue sky. Delighted, his mother opened the door and declared, 'Everything smells new.'

Danny changed into his suit. Sophie suggested not using aftershave or any hair products. Go natural, she said. Matt agreed, unable to add anything more because he was crying. He apologized.

'I can't be the crying gay guy.'

Danny kissed him on the cheek.

'Yes, you can.'

A thought popped into Danny's head. Unsure if he should suggest it.

'At the party, can you do me a favour?'

Matt nodded, of course, anything.

Danny said, 'Ask Jasper for a dance.'

# Chapter Forty-Seven

## *The Wedding*

The ceremony was to take place on the terrace, with the teak decking carefully mopped dry after the afternoon shower. Fold-out wooden seats were arranged with views over the sand dunes towards the sea. Rather than lavish flower arrangements Danny had suggested using an array of potted plants loaned from a local garden centre owned by a friend of his mother. In exchange for an invitation to the wedding she had allowed them to pack the hotel's van with violas and Sweet Williams. There had been no discussion about a theme but one seemed to emerge – a village wedding from the past. As a nod to the Olympic opening ceremony and finally able to put his theatrical stagecraft education to use, Danny made cumulus clouds out of textured Japanese *washi* paper which he curved around a wire frame and tiny battery-powered lights. These glowing clouds stood on nearly invisible supports positioned around the terrace. Rather than a classical performance with violins and cellos, they'd hired a local folk band renowned for their sell-out pub performances. The band included a tenor banjo, harmonica and accordion.

Upon arrival each guest was handed a cornflower to hold or pin to their clothes. They could sit wherever they liked. While Luis and Danny were excited about the prospect of being photographed, they opted not to have the ceremony filmed, preferring the day to remain as a series of memories and images. At three o'clock, with every guest seated, the sun made a welcome appearance and the ceremony began.

Luis stood at the front. Danny would be the one to walk out from the guest house and down the aisle. Danny and Luis came to this decision with very little deliberation. It seemed obvious to them. Danny would not be given away or walk accompanied. Luis would not wait with anyone beside him. The officiant would remain seated until Danny joined Luis at the front.

The folk band were given their cue and began to play an improvised arrangement. Inside the guest house Jasper checked over Danny's suit, picking at specks of fluff.

'It's time.'

Once Jasper had taken his seat Danny eyed the rain-damp terrace deck and took off his loafers, removing his ankle socks. He knew Jasper would think he had lost his mind, but he wanted to walk barefoot. Perhaps he was fearful of slipping but more likely he wanted to feel the wood underfoot. He opened the door and stepped out.

Chairs creaked, everyone turned to look and for once Danny didn't blush. He controlled the impulse to smile or grin, maintaining an expression somewhere between solemn and serene. Even though he had been warned about the intensity of the emotions, the force of them still took him by surprise. Briefly he was unsteady before finding his stride.

In Danny's hands was an antique walnut box containing the wedding bands. Crafted by the same Soho jewellery designer who had made their engagement rings, the bands were gold with the inside lined with polished pallasite rock, containing tiny amber crystals as if a starry night sky had been wrapped around their fingers. Arriving at the front Danny met Luis's eyes. Overcome, impulsively, Danny kissed Luis on the lips, causing the guests to break into premature applause. Luis wouldn't let him go, holding on to the kiss, the pair of them once again breaking with the correct order of things – as if this public kiss, in front of their family and friends, was all that was required to marry them.

The officiant joined Danny and Luis at the front, making a joke about not needing to say, 'and the grooms may now kiss'. Known to Danny's parents, he was a man in his early sixties who had officiated at many civil ceremonies in the area. When Danny and Luis met him, he had mentioned that he was gay, which made him less of a stranger.

Once the guests had settled down, he said, 'Both Danny and Luis have asked me to thank you for travelling to witness their marriage. And yes, you heard me correctly, I used the "m" word even though it could cost me my job. Let's get this out of the way. We're not waiting until spring – we're using the word marriage today.'

In a febrile mood after the early kiss the guests applauded again. A few of the Spanish attendees seemed confused by the statement, unaware that gay marriage was not yet legal in England. The officiant paused, allowing for the Spanish translation carried out by one of Luis's friends, a journalist from Madrid.

After the translation the officiant continued, 'Normally I would give a speech about not entering this union lightly. With Danny and Luis we can safely say neither of them are rushing into this. What it also means is that I'm not standing here offering advice. I'm standing here in admiration of everything they've already achieved. We are here to celebrate love. Their love for each other. Your love for them. The greatest happiness in life is knowing that you're loved and loving in return. If there's anything better, I've yet to hear of it. At Luis and Danny's request we're not going to follow the guidebook for ceremonies. They didn't want any readings or poems. They would simply like to say their vows. With one small adjustment. Danny and Luis would like to say *two* sets of vows. These are the vows that they wish to say today and the vows they *would have* said twenty years ago if they had been allowed to marry.'

Danny went first.

'If we had married twenty years ago, I would have said something like this. Growing up I wasn't sure if I would ever fall in love let alone be married. During my darkest years I wasn't even sure if I would reach my thirtieth birthday. You saved me, Luis. And so sharing that life with you seems only fair since half of it belongs to you.'

Danny repeated the words in Spanish, receiving appreciative applause. He moved onto his second set of vows:

'Today my vows go like this. Luis, I offer to share the rest of my life with you not because of any sadness, trauma or fear of being alone. I offer to share my life because life is better and brighter with you in it. We're a team, not to endure the world, but to enjoy it. These last twenty years have been an adventure and yet it feels like our greatest adventure is about to begin.'

The officiant turned to Luis.

'Luis, you may now say your vows, starting with the vows you would've said twenty years ago.'

Luis began, 'For the vows I would have said twenty years ago I wrote only one sentence. *Who is going to love me more than you?* And the answer to that question is no one, of that I have no doubt. I had no doubt of it twenty years ago and I have no doubt of it today.'

Luis spoke these words in Spanish before switching back into English.

'For my vows today, I add only one new sentence. *Who is going to know me better?* And the answer is no one. I couldn't have said that twenty years ago because the truth is I didn't want to be known. I didn't believe I could be both known and loved. But I can say it today. Danny, no one will know me better and no one will love me more. And I can't wait to find out who we're going to be when we're married.'

With the vows finished the officiant said, 'Luis Lagana, do you promise to love, respect, comfort and protect Daniel Smith and to share with him all that you are, and all that you are yet to be?'

Luis replied in Spanish, '*Yo, Luis Lagana, te quiero a ti, Daniel Smith, como esposo; me entrego at ti y prometo serte fiel en las alegrías y en las penas, en la salud y en la enfermedad, todos los días de mi vida.*'

He translated, 'I, Luis Lagana, love you, Daniel Smith, as my husband and I give myself to you and promise to be faithful to you in joy and in sorrow, in health and in sickness, for all the days of my life.'

The officiant turned to Danny.

'Dear Daniel.'

For some wonderful reason it felt right and natural for this man he hardly knew to address him as 'dear'.

'Do you promise to love, respect, comfort and protect Luis Lagana and to share with him all that you are and all that you are yet to be?'

Danny let the moment run, not for the drama, since his reply was inevitable, but to hold on to these few seconds. He considered using a different formulation of words, words that no one else had ever used, unconventional words, un-expected words, but what other words were there to say? These were everybody's words, and they were no less special for it. They were special because of it.

'I do.'

# Epilogue

On 29 March 2014 the first gay marriages took place in England and Wales. At the stroke of midnight John Coffey and Bernardo Martí were married in Westminster; Sean Adl-Tabatabai and Sinclair Treadway were married in Camden; and Peter McGraith and David Cabreza were married in Islington after having been a couple for seventeen years.

In Wales Federico Podeschi and Darren Williams became the nation's first gay couple to marry at a ceremony in Swansea's Civic Centre.

In Scotland, on 31 December 2014, Joe Schofield and Malcolm Brown were married at the stroke of midnight, among the first in the country, having been together for nine years.

In Northern Ireland gay marriage remained illegal until 2020.

In Spain same-sex marriage was legalized in 2005, with

the first gay marriage taking place on 11 July in the Madrid municipality of Tres Cantos between Emilio Menéndez and Carlos Baturín, a couple who had lived together for more than thirty years.

# Acknowledgements

This novel wouldn't exist without the support of my editor, Suzanne Baboneau. Suzanne's notes were crucial, but as importantly, she gave me the confidence I needed. I am not sure I believed my own stories were worth telling. Underneath the simplicity of this story were a multitude of challenges. I simply wouldn't have managed it without Suzanne. The title of the novel could also refer to our professional relationship, since we have been working together for nearly twenty years. She has been the wisest mind and the best friend any writer could hope for. And if this reads like a dedication, more than an acknowledgement, I'm sure Panagiotis won't mind.

Special thanks to my agent Mitch Hoffman at the Aaron Priest Agency in New York who, along with Suzanne, believed in this novel from the outset. His devotion to the novel has often left me lost for words, so I'm pleased to have a chance to fully express these feelings here. Mitch read and annotated multiple drafts, each time with enormous care, acting as much as a second editor as an agent. Few agents would support any book to this degree and I'm profoundly grateful for everything he's done. Mitch asked for additional insights from Natalie Rosselli at the Aaron Priest Agency, and her remarks and feedback were invaluable.

I've known Ian Chapman since *Child 44* was published. Not only is he the kindest and most wonderful man, but he has also been one of the greatest champions of my writing. He didn't blink at the change in subject matter or genre. It is only at the end of this process that I truly realize how lucky I've been.

A few close readers gave feedback on early drafts of this novel. My friend James Hopkirk, whom I have known since school, read a very early draft. He was so insightful, in part because he knows me, and knows how much this novel means to me. But mostly because he's a great reader. His notes made an enormous difference.

I'm grateful to Lars and My Blomgren who have given me so much support, connecting me with some wonderful readers who have shared their experiences of marriage. In fact, over the years writing this novel, so many people shared their experiences of marriage and love. I'm grateful to all of them. A special mention should go to Lucas Tejwani and Tudor Havriliuc, whose perspectives I cherish.

*Acknowledgements*

I would like to thank the remarkable team at my publisher Simon & Schuster UK. Thanks to Phoebe Morgan and John Sugar, who have done an incredible job working on the manuscript and bringing this book to life.

Finally, thanks to my partner Panagiotis Ladas, to whom the book is dedicated. His kindness knows no bounds and he has made home life such a joy that, after the loneliness and sadness of lockdown, writing has become a pleasure again.

# Child 44

Tom Rob Smith

**The multimillion-copy international bestseller**

MOSCOW, 1953.

Under Stalin's terrifying regime, families live in fear. When the all-powerful State claims there is no such thing as crime, who dares disagree?

An ambitious secret police officer, Leo Demidov believes he's helping to build the perfect society. But when he uncovers evidence of a killer at large – a threat the state won't admit exists – Demidov must risk everything, including the lives of those he loves, in order to expose the truth.

But what if the danger isn't from the killer he is trying to catch, but from the country he is fighting to protect?

AVAILABLE IN PAPERBACK, EBOOK AND AUDIO

**SIMON &
SCHUSTER**

# London Spy

Tom Rob Smith

**This volume of complete scripts is a
companion to the hit BBC One series starring
Ben Whishaw and Jim Broadbent**

A gripping, contemporary and emotional thriller
that tells the story of a chance romance between
two people from very different worlds.

Danny – gregarious, hedonistic and
romantic – falls in love with the enigmatic
and brilliant Alex. Then Alex disappears.

When Danny finds Alex's body, he is forced
to pursue the truth behind his death.

AVAILABLE IN PAPERBACK AND EBOOK

**SIMON &
SCHUSTER**